Loving The Small-Town Preacher's Son

A Small-Town Novel

Carla Swafford

Praise for Carla Swafford

"This savage contemporary is filled with action, deception, and emotional and sexual tension that leave readers panting right up until the highly anticipated climax."

— Publishers Weekly, starred review, for
Hidden Heat

"Exciting and breathtaking. Carla Swafford is an up-and-coming author not to be missed!"

— Sherrilyn Kenyon, *New York Times* bestselling author

"Great writing and a truly wonderful love story. Will definitely buy [m]ore books from this author."

— Reviewer on Amazon, starred review, for
Fake Play

"...dark, erotic and dangerous... "

— *RT BOOKreviews*, starred review, for
Circle of Desire

Ebook ISBN: 978-1-956518-07-8

Paperback ISBN: 978-1-956518-08-5

Hardcover ISBN: 978-1-956518-09-2

Chapter One

Mary Hightower cringed when the man swung at Luke Blackwood, the proverbial preacher's son. A pure troublemaker.

Unable to move her attention from the scene being played outside the restaurant, she placed an elbow on the table and leaned closer to the window. Hand over her mouth both in an effort to keep quiet and feeling a little ashamed by her fascination, she ignored the other patrons in Bill's Diner and waited for the fight's outcome across the street.

After ducking the roundhouse blow, Luke jabbed his shoulder into Chet Macon's gut. They tumbled onto the ground and a thick cloud of red dust billowed around their twisting bodies. Flinching, she sympathized as they would sport some bad bruises before day's end, not only from the beating, but from landing on hard clay.

She wondered what had started the fight. One moment the two men were talking and then the next Chet had punched Luke with an uppercut, delivering a good blow.

Deep inside, she had to admit seeing two well-built men

duke it out was on the naughty side of hot. She'd seen many fights in boxing rings and hockey ice rinks while living in Las Vegas, but when two alpha males brawled out in the wild, it sent a thrill throughout her body.

Followed quickly by guilt. A proper lady didn't rejoice over such savagery, her mother's voice echoed in her mind.

Who said she was the Sunday school type? Besides, her mom never followed her own advice.

A disgusted huff erupted from one of the elderly ladies sitting in the next booth.

Mary dropped her hand and slid down a little in the booth.

Betsy Twilldale and Sue Marie Coleman had met weekly for lunch and gossip at the diner for more than ten years. They always commandeered the same high-backed booth next to the plate-glass window facing Main Street and near the takeout counter to watch the comings and goings of Sand City's good citizens. Betsy and Sue Marie knew everybody and everybody's business.

Bill's Diner remained the only local meat-and-three restaurant in town, there being a couple of fast-food joints at the edge of town near the interstate. If it weren't for Susan Reed, co-owner of the diner and Bill's sister, and her wonderful chicken and dressing, Mary would never come into the place during the gossips' tête-à-têtes. But she'd been in a hurry, not aware of their presence on this particular day, until it was too late as the other tables were occupied. So she remained stuck, slumped in her seat behind the two women until Susan's next pan of dressing came out of the oven.

Their conversation drifted over to Mary's table.

"I don't care what you believe. Luke's only acting out to embarrass his daddy. I feel so sorry for Reverend Blackwood. You know they say that boy is crazy. At one time, Chet was one of his best friends." Mary recognized Sue Marie's voice and could see in her mind's eye the woman's double chin wobbling in indignation.

"He does have the devil in him," Betsy said in her prim and proper tone. "Look at him. He's smiling like it's all a big joke."

Mary had to agree as Luke was grinning like he didn't have a lick of sense. She covered her mouth again, hiding her smile as she watched Luke stand, jerk up Chet, and hit him again. They stumbled apart.

"He's a hoodlum, always has been and always will be," Betsy said, emphasizing each word with a rap on the table. "Where is that lazy sheriff?"

Then their view was blocked. A young fellow had stepped front and center to watch the fight. Most of the outside spectators stood to the side, leaving the restaurant's front window unobstructed for the older ladies' viewing pleasure.

Betsy tapped on the window until a tall farmhand grabbed the man's sleeve and jabbed his thumb toward the ladies. The poor man paled and skedaddled out of the way. Everyone knew to interfere with Betsy and Sue Marie's primary reason for living would condemn the felon to the top of the ladies' most-interested-in list.

Mary knew all about that. Since arriving in Sand City roughly eighteen months ago, she'd been the bright shining star on that list.

"Here comes Bubba now," Sue Marie said. Her vinyl seat squeaked as she moved nearer to the window. "He took his time getting here to stop this ruckus."

Mary pressed her shoulder hard to the glass to get a better angle. She crossed her fingers that her seat didn't creak like Sue Marie's. About that time, the khaki-uniformed sheriff reached the fighting men.

"I never understood how such a Christian man like the good Reverend Blackwood could rear a devil's spawn like Luke," Betsy lamented.

"Do you think Bubba's going to arrest him this time?" Sue Marie's voice filled with regret.

"Nope." Betsy popped the word. She sounded certain of the outcome.

Mary bit her lip to stop from asking why as she watched Bubba hold his hands out in supplication, talking and taking cautious steps toward Luke.

Crouched down, hands fisted, Luke's attention darted between the two men. The stockier Chet shouted at the sheriff and pointed at Luke.

"I swear Luke has something on Bubba," Betsy said in a conspiratorial whisper. "When I voted for him to be sheriff, I expected him to uphold the law no matter his personal feelings. I believe that young man needs a talking to. He needs to remember who pays his salary. Look at them arguing. How embarrassing."

Mary's gaze returned to Luke. Thick dark hair hung around his face. He wasn't smiling any longer. He remained vigilant of the people nearby, but continued to watch the other two men argue.

He appeared different from when he stopped to help her last week. Wearing nice navy-blue slacks with matching shirt and tie, he'd been polite and soft spoken while changing the flat tire, his eyes rarely meeting hers but never drifting down to her chest. By comparison, the few times she'd spoken to the sheriff or Chet, they'd stared at her breasts as if she wore tassels.

"You do have to admit, devil's spawn or not, he's awfully

pretty," Sue Marie said like a star-struck teenager. "That dark hair and eyes. Ruth told me last week she saw him cutting the Reverend's grass and he was shirtless. He had muscles you only see on those romance novels Ruth loves to read."

A giggle almost escaped before Mary bit her bottom lip. The last thing she needed was to get caught eavesdropping. Maybe there was hope for Sue Marie.

"She should be ashamed of herself. He's young enough to be her son." Betsy paused. From the jingle of ice, Mary guessed the thin woman had taken a sip of her drink. Gossiping was thirsty business. "He probably didn't have anything better to do than work out in the prison yard. I heard they have all the comforts of home."

"I have no idea," Sue Marie said as if something else had caught her attention. "Look at that."

Betsy stood and Mary slumped further down in her booth.

"Bubba's arresting Chet. That just doesn't make sense." Betsy's disgust sharpened each word. "That does it. I've got to talk to that young man and see why he's running scared of Luke."

"Mary? Your order is ready," Susan said loud enough so every customer could hear. The woman stared straight at her with the corners of her mouth fighting a grin.

Oh, crap.

Mary placed a finger over her lips. The woman had a wicked sense of humor that Mary normally enjoyed but this wasn't one of those times.

"Better come and get it before it gets cold. You know how your mom feels about that." Susan blinked several times, wide-eyed, pretending innocence. "Mary?" She lifted the white bag with Mary's order.

"Is that you, Mrs. Hightower?" Sue Marie craned her neck around the booth, watching Mary scramble from between the table and high-backed bench.

As she stood, she felt gangly towering over the seated rotund Sue Marie. At the same time, the weed-thin Betsy eyed her as if Mary planned to strip in the middle of the diner. Heavens, responding to her fake last name was a big win at this point.

"Why, hello, Mrs. Hightower." The tone Betsy used said she doubted the respectable title. "I was just telling Sue Marie earlier that you grew up in Birmingham."

"Yes and then we moved to Las Vegas when I turned fifteen." How could she get away without being rude? She didn't want to provide more gossip than necessary.

"I also told her how your husband, bless his soul, had died right before you came to town. That you even brought him with you and buried him in Sand City's finest cemetery. I thought that was so romantic," Betsy said, pronouncing each syllable of the last word.

Sue Marie's head and chin bobbed in agreement.

Romantic? They had a perverse way of thinking what was romantic.

Feeling more uneasy by the minute and wanting out of there, she did what she'd learned a long time ago, she smiled —cheeks aching—and nodded, hoping her silence would end the torture sooner.

"How are you and your mama enjoying living at old Samuel Hicks's place?" Betsy sat with her hands primly placed in her lap and continued her remarks. "I'd imagine for a city girl like you, living so far out in that big rambling house can be rather boring. Especially after living in wild Sinful City for so many years."

Sinful City? That's Sin City. Whatever. Mary restrained

from rolling her eyes. *Oh my, what was the woman getting to?*

Sue Marie's head bobbed once again like a bobblehead doll on a car's dashboard.

Mary began to edge away, hoping she could grab her food and get out of the door before she said something she'd regret. Did her smile look as plastic as it felt?

"I'm just amazed that someone with your sophistication would want to live in the backwoods of Alabama." Betsy opened her eyes wide, all innocence. "Bless your heart."

Had she just been insulted by an expert?

"If you ladies would excuse me, Mom's waiting for dinner and I hate for it to get cold." She dipped her head and walked to the counter. Mary could still hear the old gossips. Either their hearing was poor or they didn't care, probably a little of both.

Her mom always said there had to be benefits to growing old, and not caring what others thought of a person should be one and the other was speaking the bare truth, if the others wanted to hear it or not.

"She does dress mighty extra for a small town. Must be her way of flaunting her money. I've never seen shoes like that at Lee's Dress and Shoe Barn." Sue Marie said the last almost with a mouthful of envy.

Mary sighed and handed a twenty to Susan. Her shoulders burned from the stares drilling into her back. She raised an eyebrow at Susan as the woman moved as if she was born half sloth.

Why in the world was Susan opening another roll of quarters? She had a slot full now.

One Jimmy Choo-clad foot tapping, Mary glared at her friend. A soon to be ex-friend at this rate. Susan grinned bigger and took her ever-loving time in making change.

"You're a cruel, cruel person, Susan Reed," she whispered.

"I couldn't resist. Those two biddies keep me in the know, not counting entertained. Really, they're harmless." Susan chuckled and slowly counted out the change, grinning in near maniacal pleasure the whole time.

Mary gave a long-suffering sigh, causing Susan to chuckle again. If not for her years of experience on stage, she'd faint from embarrassment.

"No righteous woman would wear shoes like that. She's not Baptist. Otherwise, you and I would see her at church. I asked around. She doesn't go to Valley Presbyterian or Rock Spring Methodist. I could tell by the way she dressed and walked she's a heathen." Betsy huffed in righteous indignation.

"I sure like her shoes," Sue Marie said with longing. "Tiger-striped pumps. Who would've thought? I wonder if they're real tiger skin? They're not too high-heeled and look so comfortable." With a quick glance toward the booth, Mary thought Sue Marie talked and stared at her shoes enough to break more than one commandment.

Once Susan handed over her order and change, Mary clutched the paper bag with white knuckles and turned toward the door. Holding her head high, she smiled at the two women. "Have a good day, ladies. By the way, Sue Marie, I bought the shoes in New York at Saks and they're imitation."

"Goodness gracious," Betsy and Sue Marie said as one.

When Mary finally reached the sidewalk, she inhaled, taking a deep breath of fresh air to calm her nerves. She'd moved to Sand City to become part of the tight community and to feel secure in the neighbor-looking-after-neighbor mentality. But the two old women were the stuff of small town nightmares.

Thankfully, Sand City had more good people than not, and she loved living there. She refused to think about the women trying to ruin her day as she headed toward her car.

Almost there, she spotted Luke coming in her direction. His loose-limbed walk made her think of the old western she'd watched the other night. Yeah. He looked like a gunfighter walking through town, shoulders straight and hands ready for action at his sides, daring anyone to stop him.

Heaven help her, she had enough to worry about with her mom's recently diagnosed Alzheimer's, and just because he'd been kind to help her with the tire...well, that was why she'd let her mom talk her into hiring him as their handyman.

Her mom possessed a talent for laying on guilt trips so thickly Mary often wondered how she survived the weight. To be fair, with all the poor decisions she'd made over the years, she couldn't blame her mom.

A short distance from her Lexus, she heard, "Ms. Hightower."

Her heart jumped. His deep drawl brought wonderful shivers through her body.

Swallowing, she seriously considered pretending she hadn't heard. But her mother hadn't reared a coward. So she made sure to plaster on a casual smile as she turned.

"Hello, Mr. Blackwood."

Dust covered his dark hair as it straggled over one masculine brow. Her fingertips burned to move the strands out of the way. She pressed the bag closer to her chest as her nails dug into the paper, certain they'd leave scorch marks. Everything about him screamed danger but she still found herself drawn. If he ever discovered how his mere presence affected her…no. She refused to be attracted to him. There was nothing attractive about trouble.

And he oozed a ton of it. She no longer wanted that in her life. She wanted peace and quiet. Whenever she decided to date again, it would be with a good man. One who had a nine-to-five job. A safe man. A boring man.

Wait, not boring. Crap.

A hand with bruised knuckles tossed the bothersome hair from his eyes. "I want to apologize for what you saw in front of the diner. I never start—"

"I saw Chet swing first." She bit her bottom lip and looked away. Admitting she understood why he fought with Chet would only encourage his interest in her. Her gaze landed on the large window of the diner. The two old biddies shook their heads as they watched them.

She sighed. Bringing more attention to herself was the last thing she needed.

"Excuse me, but I need to get home before the food's cold," she said, raising the sack as if she needed proof.

He cleared his throat.

"I wanted to make sure it's okay for me to bring a few supplies over Sunday after church. That'll make it easier to start painting first thing Monday morning." Those beautiful dark eyes darted away as soon as they met hers.

"Sure. We have a couple of ladders if you need them. I believe we have only one drop cloth." Why did his nervousness make her nervous? Her gaze shot toward her Lexus as she shifted the food. She really wanted to leave.

Her fingers ached from their grip, and she consciously loosened them enough to allow circulation to return. When he kept quiet, she glanced back.

His gaze had drifted down her body.

Many men over the years had stared at her, but not the way he did. His warm gaze made her feel different. As if he wanted to wrap her in cotton and only bring her out for special occasions. As if she was unique.

"I'll need at least three more. If you have some old bed sheets, they'll do." He looked at his feet and hunched his shoulders.

Bed? Oh, yes, the drop cloths for painting.

"That's a good idea. I'll see what I can find." Something about hearing the word "bed" from his lips caused her face to warm. Feeling like a shy teenager—had she'd ever been so young—she took a deep breath before she said, "I'll see you Sunday."

As he nodded, a breeze blew the strands of hair into his face again. The musky scent of hot male skin drifted over her. Every bit of her willpower centered on not closing her eyes and inhaling. She loved men. Everything about them, but she'd sworn off all males until she got her mom settled in the new town.

"Yeah. Good afternoon, Mrs. Hightower."

She looked at his five o'clock shadow, broad shoulders, bruised knuckles and chin, and long, long legs encased in faded jeans. What was it about him that caused her body to buzz with energy? How long since she'd felt such an attraction?

It had been when she met her husband. Something about a bad boy got her blood to flowing.

Correct that. Bad man.

Those she'd definitely sworn off.

"Good afternoon." She barely let the words pass her lips before she was hurrying to her car.

She shoved her bag onto the passenger seat and then backed out the car. One glance in the rearview mirror proved Luke stood on the sidewalk, watching as she drove away. He looked so forlorn with his hair in his face and his hands shoved into his denim pockets. Her heart ached for the loneliness she sensed in the hunched posture.

No. She refused to go down that slippery slope again. He didn't need her to save him. She'd learned the hard way bad boys, especially bad men, should save themselves. Besides, she needed no man to fulfill her life. There was nothing about a man she missed.

The forbidden thought of hair-rough masculine legs rubbing along hers in the middle of the night jolted her into returning her attention to the road. Sure, having a man in her lonely bed made the nights a lot shorter, but was it worth the trouble they caused?

Time to keep her mind on the business at hand. Take care of her mother and avoid any scandals. The last thing she needed was word getting to Las Vegas about her settling in the small Alabama town. She wanted to avoid the life she'd left behind catching up with her. Anyway, she'd promised her mom they'd start over. No turning back. And she'd done everything she could think of to make sure of that.

On that thought, as her Lexus passed the Sand City Cemetery, she stared straight ahead. She gripped the steering wheel and refused to look at her husband's white headstone not far off the main road. Merely ten feet from the statue of a sleeping lamb, it glinted accusingly in the warm September sun.

Yes. She'd done everything she could.

Chapter Two

Luke hungrily watched the Lexus pull away.

He inhaled. Whatever fragrance she wore lingered in the air. Everything about her reminded him of honeysuckle and light breezes.

How he wished he could stay around that woman twenty-four-seven. Pretty, but not beautiful, her presence always soothed him. He nodded. Yeah, that was how he felt around her. Calm and relaxed.

The ever-present knot in his gut eased up whenever she came close. The urge to punch a wall or pummel a person dissolved with one glimpse of her long legs and gentle smile. Sure, he acted like a tongue-tied idiot around her but that never stopped him from thinking up excuses to be near.

As to painting inside her house, how hard could it be? Handling a roller and brush was a lot easier than the tedious duty of picking up trash along the highway or fearing for his life each time he'd stepped out of his jail cell.

From the way she fidgeted and held herself, he knew he made her nervous. She probably thought he wanted to jump her bones. Yeah, well, he did, but she deserved better than the likes of him.

He looked at his work-rough hands. Bruised and cut, they always looked battered and scarred, nothing like a normal human's. Rubbing his hands against his jeans, he knew there was no hope. No matter how many times he scrubbed them, he could still see blood coating every inch. Sticky between his fingers, the metallic stench was more than he could stomach. No way would a babe like her be interested in an ex-con and small town hick.

He fooled no one.

Luke shook his head, sticking his hands into his back pockets. Nothing else to do but head back to the Sandbox. The bar sported two pool tables and had become his second home. His buddies, Evil and Smooth, should be waiting for him.

Shouting mixed with the never-ending thump of the jukebox vibrated through his body as he entered the dark room. The sweet yeast smell of beer teased his nostrils, promising a night of forgetfulness. He nodded at the bartender as he weaved his way around tables and chairs to the pool table nearest the back door. Evil and Smooth were arguing about whose turn it was to break the racked balls.

"It's my turn." Luke grabbed a pool stick and shoved Smooth to the side.

"Hey, man, I heard you kicked Chet's flat ass." Evil grinned as he leaned against the wall and waited his turn.

"Flat ass? You mean fat ass, you idiot." The dishwater blond, Smooth, jabbed his brother's arm.

"Sometimes you hear wrong." Luke struck the white ball and watched as a solid green one rolled into a corner and a yellow into the side pocket. The sound was almost as satisfying as his fist hitting Chet's face. No. He refused to think about it. He hated the elation that fighting gave him. It was wrong. One day, he'd learn how to ignore Chet's insults.

"Don't tell me he kicked yours?" Evil stood straight, his black brows raised.

Before Luke could answer, Smooth piped up. "I heard Bubba stopped the fight."

Luke lined up his next shot as his stomach rolled. Couldn't they find another subject and leave him to enjoy the pool game? The solid blue went into the corner.

"Hell, since you're here, I guess that means Bubba didn't arrest you." Evil leaned his shoulders against the wall once more and crossed his tattooed arms. "What did you do, suck his dick?"

Eyeing the balls on the table, Luke raised his middle finger over his shoulder at Evil. He didn't take it personally, the brothers loved teasing anyone who hung out with them. Truth be known, besides himself, Luke didn't know of anyone else in Sand City who was their friend.

A solid red bounced off the cushioned side and dropped into an opposite side pocket.

"I also heard that Bubba arrested Chet," Smooth added.

"Shit, man, you've got the luck of the devil." Evil chuckled.

"No luck to it. End of story." He narrowed his eyes, lining up the shot. Why wouldn't they just shut up? Considering his friends were also few and far between, he didn't say anything, but tapped the burgundy ball toward the corner nearest Smooth. It clicked against the orange ball as it was going in and then the second one dropped in too.

Smooth looked up, eyes wide, and shook his head as he mouthed "wow."

About two years ago, after he'd been released from St.

Clair Correctional, they had covered his back in a fight at the Sandbox. They'd been friends ever since. He'd remembered the Rogan brothers from high school. A few years older—one was blond like an angel and the other as dark as a demon—they thought nothing of stirring up trouble. They had disappeared after graduation and reappeared not long before he came back home.

He shot the last solid, the purple one, into a side pocket and then aimed for the black. The white went awry and slipped into a pocket before the black dropped in the corner.

"Damn devil's fickle luck." Evil began to rack the balls for another game.

Yeah, that's his luck. Never consistent. And since the age of twelve, mostly bad.

Luke leaned against the wall, drinking his beer as he watched Evil and Smooth play the next game. They all had something in common. They'd lost their mothers at a young age. Instead of dying as his mom had, the brothers' mom had just up and disappeared. Their dad claimed she took up with a carny man from the local fair and left town in a truck loaded down with Kewpie dolls.

More than likely, the brothers' mom had gotten tired of being a punching bag for their old man. What a shame she hadn't taken her kids. Their father had moved on to the boys until they started fighting back and moved out.

"Hey, dirt bag, you and me are going to talk." Chet walked over with his two football-player-sized cousins close behind. Obviously, Bubba only held him for a couple of hours in the hope he'd cool down.

Luke placed the pool stick to the side. He couldn't afford replacing any more sticks. The owner had just recently allowed him and the boys to enter the bar again after the last fight three months earlier.

"Let's take it outside." Luke turned toward the back door. Elation washed over him. At least a good fight would take the edge off. It was the next best thing to tasting every inch of Mary Hightower in those tiger-striped shoes.

<<<>>>

Luke shivered in the cool evening breeze, mindlessly petting the donkey he'd recently adopted.

What kind of sicko stood across a field to watch shadows flit past curtains at a neighbor's house? When he'd heard a woman and her elderly mother had bought the Hicks place nearby, he imagined two white-haired old women. Then a week later he spotted Mary. Gussied up in a little black dress with some type of wide-brimmed hat, she looked like one of those old-time movie stars. He could imagine her driving a red '59 Cadillac convertible.

He heard the back screen door creak before his dad's deep voice reached out to him.

"Hey, son, come in and I'll doctor those cuts."

The Reverend Ezekiel Blackwood looked more like a prize fighter than a man of God. Broad shoulders and craggy face, he stood a good six-foot-five, two inches taller than his son, and sported a full head of hair with plenty of silver strands. Retired from the Missionary Baptist Church in nearby Marystown, his dad kept busy helping out at the local homeless shelter and praying that his son wouldn't make any more stupid mistakes.

Luke gave a final pat to the animal and then climbed over the wooden fence and loped to the kitchen door. His dad stepped back as he entered and the door clacked shut behind them. Bandages, cotton, and hydrogen peroxide waited on the table. He took a chair and watched his dad settle across from him.

"I'll start with your knuckles."

His big hands gently pulled Luke's over the table between them. He worked without fuss, grimacing whenever Luke hissed at a particularly nasty cut.

Everyone told him how fortunate he was to have such a wonderful father, a good man for a dad. They were right. His dad deserved a better son. The sadness in the old man's eyes made his chest ache. He wanted to tell his dad that everything would be okay, only he'd be lying.

Luke stretched out his legs and bumped his dad's beneath the table. He sat straighter and pulled his legs back. When he was twelve, everyone could tell he'd be as tall as his dad. His mom had teased them about being all legs and not giving her room to stretch her stubby ones. She'd had such a great sense of humor. He'd always wondered what she would've done if she'd been alive when he went to the pen.

His dad had stood alone by his side when Luke had been arrested for burglary and sent to prison. He never asked him if he was guilty or not. They'd made plenty of mistakes since his mom died. They were stuck with their own demons. Not talking about it was their way of dealing with it all.

"This looks deep enough to scar. You need to get the doctor to look at it. Probably needs a couple stitches," his dad said as he placed the last butterfly bandage on a cut near his eye.

Luke stood and shook his head. What's another scar? He headed toward his bedroom.

"Son."

Without turning, Luke stopped with his head down. He wanted to run, to not listen to his dad's defeated tone. It crushed him to hear it.

"I had hoped that you would've realized by now what happened wasn't your fault."

Luke shook his head again and continued toward his bedroom. The tension he'd released during the fight returned full force. Hands fisted, he resisted the urge to slam the door behind him. His anger was directed more at himself than his dad. What had the prison doc said? Oh, yeah, he needed to find his own place and start looking at the future and less at the past.

Easier said than done.

He chucked his boots, stripped jeans and shirt, and dumped them on the floor before falling in bed to stare at the four walls. Bare of all mementos from his childhood, the spartan room held only a bed, a night stand with a lamp, and a chest of drawers.

So different than when his mom was alive. The whole house had changed. All the warmth had seeped out. At first, his father had tried to keep everything like before, but unfortunately the cooking and cleaning fell on Luke's twelve-year-old shoulders. He learned. Mostly the hard way.

His mom had died not more than fifteen feet from where he lay. He knew if he lifted the rug beneath the coffee table in the living room, the stain would still be there. The blood never faded from the wood, no matter what they used to clean it. Uncomfortable with the direction of his thoughts, he forced the past to the shadows in his mind.

Palms flat against his head, he squeezed his temples as if he could push in happy thoughts. Anything pleasant. Something worth lying in bed, and possibly helped him to go to sleep, that promised to bring sweet dreams.

Mary Hightower.

Yeah. She invoked thoughts that shoved the bad ones away. He bet all her curves were real and silky smooth. He recalled her smell and thought about summer mornings and honeysuckle hanging over a fence.

He was captivated by how she moved, like every woman should, with a sway to her hips asking for her man to follow. He wished he could be that man. For certain, he would follow her to hell.

With a wry grin, he glanced at his stiffening cock and tossed the sheet across his groin.

Tomorrow he'd drop off the paint and supplies and take advantage of seeing the woman again who invaded his dreams. Besides, he'd rather dream of sex with an angel than lie awake in his own hell of regrets.

Chapter Three

"Mom, what were you thinking when you insisted I hire an ex-con to work around here?" Mary took a bite of her fluffy scrambled eggs.

Sunshine streamed in through the thin lacy curtains, bathing the kitchen in warmth the early fall Sunday morning promised.

"We need a man around here to do the nasty chores." Her mom pointed a crooked finger at her. The white curls on her head jiggled with each word.

Using her fork, her mom nudged the grits away from her eggs and toast. Mary kept an eye on how much her mother ate. Though the older woman's appetite had improved after they moved in, she noticed in the past week it had fallen off again.

Strange to think how thankful she was that her mom had lost her way in the car about two years ago. Mom had a great sense of direction. The older woman had called, sobbing, that she needed Mary to come and get her as she had no idea how to return home.

Without a second thought, Mary had quickly made her an appointment with the doctor. Her mom's health had always been near-perfect and there had to be a reason for her to forget how to get home. After many tests and several months, the doctor's diagnosis confirmed what they feared. Alice Ford was in the early stages of Alzheimer's.

Coming to this farm and living in a house similar to her mom's childhood home seemed a good idea at the time. They could get away from an uncomfortable situation in Las Vegas by moving to the little town in Alabama and starting over. With the soft mountains of her youth surrounding her, her mom could develop a routine that would help her cope with the disease as it progressed.

"But why a convict? Why Luke?"

"Who?" Her mom looked up from her food to stare at her with a blank expression.

"Luke Blackwood. The man we hired to do chores around here."

Mary's fingers whitened around the fork's handle as she placed it on her plate. Was the blank stare from the disease or a typical expression anyone would give another while lost in thought? Mary hated how the disease had colored all her thoughts and responses to her mom.

"Oh. The young man that lives across the field." Her mom's face brightened.

"Yes." Mary released her breath. Her mom remembered.

"We can't keep up the work around here. Every farm needs a man and you're in no hurry to find one. So I found one for you."

Mary searched the beloved face across the table. Did she mean find a man to work the farm or find a man to be in her life? Surely, her mom hadn't forgotten the husband she'd buried just eighteen months ago. After Vincent died, they had moved as quickly as the sale of their Las Vegas homes allowed. She had found the farm through the internet and her mom insisted on her buying it. Once she contacted the real estate salesperson, the woman couldn't process the paperwork fast enough.

"I don't need a full-time handyman. We can always hire a different professional for each job." She placed her hand on the wrinkled one across from her. "We have plenty of money and can afford it."

"But do you really want to use *that* money?"

"I earned it." She released her mother's hand and sat back.

She'd rather not argue but refused to be ashamed of how she'd earned the money. Dancing in the Vegas shows had been hard work, and she deserved every penny plus more, and the money Vincent left came from a job that actually killed him. Not spending it meant his life was overvalued, and it had never been that.

"What's the harm?" the older woman asked. "I bet he's great in the sack."

Mary jerked her attention back to her mother. "Mom! Why are you talking like that?"

The tingling on her face warned her she was blushing. Her mom delighted in teasing her, and at times, could be a nuisance with it.

"Don't tell me a big girl like you hasn't wondered? With those long legs, just out of bed whiskers, and shaggy hair... hmm, hmm. You always liked bad boys."

Unsure of why her mom wanted to push her at Luke, she shook her head. "And what did it get me? A lot of heartache and a past best forgotten. No way. Give me an accountant or any guy with a normal job."

"You can't get any more normal than a handyman." Her mom grinned and placed a fork full of eggs into her mouth.

"Well, I'm not in a hurry to date, so I don't believe we have to worry." She refused to let her mom bait her further on the subject. Mary picked up her plate and walked to the garbage can. "Besides I don't want to replace Vinny."

Her mom muttered.

Mary rolled her eyes. She could only imagine what her mom had said as she'd never liked Vincent, and Mary understood why. His lifestyle had often involved traveling between Las Vegas and Atlantic City. When they had finally settled in Las Vegas, she had made sure Vincent built her mom a home in their neighborhood. Still, her husband and mom barely tolerated each other.

Five short years later he died and she had to move again. Leaving that life behind was one of the few good decisions she'd made since leaving home as a teenager because of her mom's boyfriend at the time. She now lived the way she'd always wanted. Normal. And, hopefully, one day, a normal life with a normal man.

She stared out the kitchen window toward the small, white clapboard house across the field.

No matter how handsome and sexy or how his dark-blue eyes lightened when he looked at her, Luke was a bad boy. Last thing she wanted was to become mixed up in his world.

She'd barely escaped with her life from the last one.

Mary moved out of the kitchen into the living room. No way would she admit her restlessness was caused by a tall, lanky bad boy who stirred a need she wanted to deny. As if she'd conjured him up, she eyed a green truck with a yellow rear fender rattling up the long, curvy drive. The sun shone through the cracked windshield detailing every inch of the devilishly good-looking face of the man behind the steering wheel. The way the light glistened off his hair, it revealed his true color of chestnut, bringing out the deep reds and auburns that would go unnoticed on a cloudy day.

When the truck slowed to a stop in front of the house, she stepped into the shadows of the living room between the door and a curtained window. She hoped she'd gone unnoticed through the screen door.

"Is that Luke?"

Mary gasped and covered her racing heart. Her mom was too light on her feet. She weighed thirty pounds more than Mary, and at an inch below her five-foot-seven height, her mom should be easy to spot.

"Yes, ma'am." One hand on her chest to calm down her heart, Mary nudged the curtain a sliver to the side.

"Well, quit gawking at the boy and invite him in. My water's boiling and once the leaves have seeped, I'll stir up plenty of iced tea." Her mom returned to the kitchen.

She watched the muscles tighten in his forearms as he lifted a ladder and placed it near the walkway and then returned to the back of his truck. She leaned back, her eyes remaining on the lean handyman, and spoke loud enough to be heard in the kitchen.

"He's not working today. You know it's Sunday. He'll be back tomorrow."

"I know that. I remember growing up in Alabama. No one works on Sunday if they can help it." Her mom slammed a cabinet door. "Who says he can't have a glass of sweet tea today?"

Mary sighed and stepped back to the screen door. They had left the front door open to enjoy the mild day, while leaving the wire screen closed to keep bird-sized mosquitoes from darting in. When she reached for the handle, she found him standing on the other side of the wire screen with a bucket in each hand and sacks clinched beneath both arms.

They stared at each other. The shade of the front porch softened his sharp features and darkened his hair further. With the screen between them, he appeared to be part of a dream. A little blurred and untouchable.

"Do you want me to leave it out here or inside?" he asked.

When he raised the buckets, she realized she'd been staring without saying a word.

"Uh, yeah."

"For goodness' sake, Mary, let the boy in!"

Heat bloomed on her face as she opened the door and stepped to the side. How long had she stared? Just because he looked different than the men she'd become accustomed to—smooth-talking high-rollers wearing thousand-dollar suits—didn't mean she had to make a fool of herself.

"Which room did you want me to start with?" He glanced through the doorways leading to the formal dining and living rooms. When she didn't answer, he held up a paint can and then scrabbled to catch a bag before it hit the floor.

She reached forward to help and quickly straightened, embarrassed by how close her face had gotten to his chest. A masculine eyebrow lifted when his attention returned to her.

"Room?" He hesitated and then said, "Which room should I start with? I thought it best to leave the supplies there."

"Uh, the family room and then the kitchen. They're worse for wear." Worse for wear? Her southernisms had returned with a vengeance since settling in Sand City.

A crooked grin revealed a small dimple near the corner of his mouth. *Oh, yes.* The man was dangerous to her decision of staying away from his type.

He shifted his load and cleared his throat, that crooked grin returning.

What was wrong with her? Obviously, it'd been a long while since she'd spent time with a man. Still no excuse to act like an ignoramus.

"Of course, this way." She pointed through the formal dining room to another door.

"Hey, Luke." Her mother's eyes glinted in amusement. Obviously she'd been listening to her act like a tongue-tied teenager. "You can place your stuff in that spot." She pointed to a space between an end table and the large picture window. "I expect you around seven tomorrow for breakfast."

"No need, ma'am. I always have breakfast before I feed the livestock at five. If you'll excuse me, I'm fixing to drop these if I don't sit them down."

Mary held in her smile at his use of the phrase *fixing to.* Her mother said stuff like that all the time, and really she couldn't laugh after spouting the earlier one. He sounded so damn cute and sexy.

She tagged along behind him, keeping her gaze off his behind.

"How long have you had..." She waved her hand toward the back window that looked over the pasture. Could they really be described as livestock?

"The misfits." He chuckled.

"Yeah." She watched as he arranged the paints and bags on the floor. Muscles shifted beneath his T-shirt, stretching the material as his arms bulged and released with each movement. Hauling bales of hay and whatever other farm-like chores he did kept him in shape.

Fascinating.

No. Not fascinating. Bad boys are bad. Bad. And not cute and sexy.

She mentally shook her head. Dentists, doctors, and accountants were the normal regular occupations she should have on her list of prospective dates.

"The three-legged goat about two years. The earless donkey about four years and the blind mare about five months. Dad can't say no. He has a soft spot for misfits." A hurt flickered in those navy-blue eyes.

Something more was being said than she understood. She'd heard tales about Luke, but would a dad think his own son a misfit? Or was it more that his dad cared for those hurt by past events not of their making?

No. Blast it.

There she went again. She had to stop hearing more than what he told her. Reading between the lines of what a bad boy said had gotten her in more trouble over the years than she ever wanted. She refused to fall for that trap again.

"Luke, would you like a glass of iced tea?" Her mom's question brought Mary back to her senses.

Mary bit the side of her mouth. Time for her to concentrate on what was happening around her. She'd been staring. Again.

Chapter Four

Luke wanted to tell Mary so many things. That surprised him. He rarely spoke to strangers, and just barely to his two friends. If he told her how he felt, she'd know he was as crazy as everyone believed. But the need to spill his guts was so strong. Some days he was certain he could explode at any minute. With Mary, he wanted to tell her how he felt every time he saw her, being in her presence made him want to be a better man. At the same time, when he left her, the old hurts, hatreds welled up and he wanted to detonate in the worst way.

She probably had never been around an ex-con before, and expected him to go psycho.

"No, thank you anyway, Mrs. Ford. I better head over to the shelter. Dad's expecting a crowd. They're having Susan's chicken and dressing after services. That brings them off the streets like nobody's business."

From the surprised look on Mary's face, she obviously thought he'd volunteered. Was it so hard to imagine? At one time, when he was younger, he didn't mind pitching in without pay. But circumstances changed. No one in town would hire him. So his dad paid him to do odd jobs around the shelter and the small farm they owned. Luke didn't need much. He lived with his dad for goodness' sake. Wasn't like he had a girl or would ever have one. Most good women stayed away as if he carried the plague. And the bad girls...he'd had enough of their drama.

This was why the paint job was so important to him. He would make enough money to move into his own place. Evil had told him about a double-wide for rent next to theirs in Hicks's Trailer Park. Once Mrs. Ford told others what a good job he'd done, hopefully it would lead to more work.

"Then we'll see you tomorrow. Around seven?" Mrs. Ford said and glanced at Mary.

If he didn't know better, he'd think Mary's mom wanted her daughter to say something, but she remained quiet.

"Yes, ma'am," he answered, breaking the silence.

He turned to leave when he heard Mrs. Ford say, "Where's your manners, girl? Walk the boy to the door."

Coldness pressed his spine straight. "No need. I know my way."

Did they think he'd steal their china on the way out the door? He felt ashamed of the thought. He knew good Southern manners demanded the hostess see a guest off. Though the last few years had taught him people rarely trusted someone like him. Screw up once and it was all over.

The good townsfolk of Sand City could stick it in their...where the sun didn't shine as far as he cared, but he wanted Mary to trust him, to feel safe with him.

Even in her presence, he tried not to cuss in his thoughts as well as out loud. He looked up in exasperation.

That was stupid and he needed to quit worrying about it. She couldn't care less what he said or thought. But it had been drilled in him from childhood, cussing was not proper in front of women.

His dad would never believe he had a bit of restraint. So why try? She probably expected his dirty mouth. In fact, he could think of a few choice ones to whisper in her ear while he slowly fucked her.

The back of his neck heated. He felt like a slow-witted teenager around her. She always came across so sophisticated, even in the jeans and blouse she wore that afternoon.

He followed her toward the front door. The scent of honeysuckle wafted along behind her. For a second he closed his eyes and inhaled and slammed into the door.

"Oh, no." She reached out, and he stepped away. "I'm so sorry. I thought you saw the wind had partially closed the door."

Feeling like a total doofus, Luke murmured, "No problem," and rushed out to the truck as he resisted the need to rub his bruised forehead. He had a couple more cans to leave but tomorrow would do just as well. He wanted to recover some of his dignity before seeing Mary again.

Chapter Five

ary watched the truck speed down the drive until the phone rang.

"Answer that," her mom said from inside the kitchen. "I'm elbow-deep in flour. That apple cobbler isn't going to make itself. I bet Luke loves apples. Most southern boys do."

She grabbed the handset. They still had a house phone as her mom hated the pocket ones, as she called them. The telephone was an old one her mom had for years and carried from house to house. The receiver rested on a hook in the base with the dial pad and display with red letters. The ancient set included a working voicemail.

"Hello," she absentmindedly answered. Craning her neck, she watched the truck through the front window.

Maybe she should've insisted Luke wait to make certain he was okay. By the time the green and yellow speck disappeared down the road, she realized no one had said a word over the phone.

"Hello?" She glanced at the display.

A red light on the base glowed though the location

wasn't showing. The caller was still connected. She heard breathing. Not like someone trying to leave an obscene phone call by panting, or unable to speak because of fear or exercise. Whoever was on the other end had planned to scare her. She felt it to her bones. There was something about the heaviness of the breathing that made her certain it was a man. He wanted to make certain she answered, that he had called the right number.

She carefully hung up. In automaton mode, she leaned over and pressed the recall button. A seven-zero-two area code. She knew that one well. Las Vegas.

Calling back was unnecessary. Only because she knew they'd allowed her to see the number, the same number that had been important to her husband for many years.

On leaving Las Vegas, she and her mom had paid cash for the moving, left without a forwarding address, cancelled all their credit cards, and purchased the house through a paper company her husband had taught her to create.

Then again, had she really expected not to be tracked down? That they would forget her? To leave her alone after Vincent died? He'd warned her and provided protection she'd hoped to never use.

Well, she guessed she'd find out how angry his former boss became when blackmailed. She only needed to reclaim it from where it was hidden. That in itself was going to be a complication. The evidence was buried with her husband.

Chapter Six

Luke glared at the house across the pasture as he curried the blind mare. He needed to break this new bad habit of watching his neighbor. He should find a hobby or a girl. No. A woman. A woman with rich, chocolate-brown hair. With curves that softened beneath his touch and cushioned his head at night. He wanted silken thighs clasped around his waist, hell, around his neck and her purring like a kitten. His groin tightened with the image.

"Hey, Lu! Your pa said you were out here moping." Evil stretched his arms across the top of the rail, dangling his hands in the soft breeze. "Whatcha staring at?"

"Just thinking."

Out of the corner of his eye, he noticed Smooth stop a couple of steps back and shift his feet impatiently as he glanced at his older brother.

"Hey, Smooth and me are heading up to Birmingham to see a man about a job. Come with us. It promises to be enough to keep us happy for a while. Little brother and I agreed to bring you in as a partner."

Luke looked at Smooth, who nodded.

This was one of many times they'd asked him to join in their schemes. So far, he'd turned them down. The type of job Evil offered would probably land Luke back in the slammer with extended time. His parole wasn't up until June.

"I've got to pass." He looked back toward the large farmhouse.

"Man, we plan to leave tonight and go partying on the Big Ham's Southside. We don't meet up with the guy until tomorrow at noon. You can come and party with us at least." Evil nudged Luke with his shoulder and whispered, "Why don't you go and get a piece of what's keeping you here? Then meet with us in Birmingham. We'll be at Bottles Bar until two. They've got women Jell-O wrestling tonight. Call me when you reach the city limits. I'll check it a couple times for your number."

Why didn't it appeal to him? At one time, he would've jumped on it. He narrowed his eyes and cut them toward the man.

"I'm not coming." He shook his head. "I find enough trouble here without going to Birmingham to look for more."

"Bullshit." Evil chuckled and walked away. "Don't forget to call before you head there. That is, if you can pull yourself away from sniffing at that tall, fancy woman's skirts."

Luke shook his head and led the mare to the barn. Evil had it wrong. Staying in Sand City had nothing to do with Mary. Well, not much. He looked at the house again and watched as the curtains lit up in what he guessed to be her bedroom.

He bet she had a nice big, soft bed. That honeysuckle

and a clean, early morning breeze scent probably filled the room.

What craziness had him standing around dreaming about a woman's bedroom?

Someone as beautiful and sophisticated as Mary would never think twice about someone like him. Until this morning, she acted as if he touched her, she would scream. Damn biddies. They probably told her all about his past and how he killed his mother.

Chapter Seven

Mary sighed. The clock on her nightstand read eleven-eleven and she still couldn't sleep. Earlier, when she crawled into bed, she'd wanted to think of anything but Las Vegas and the phone call that morning. Dreaming of Luke had been the best foil. Lean back muscles and long runner's legs. She wanted to pull the white T-shirt off dream-Luke and lick every dip between each muscle, to taste his straight serious lips as she encouraged the corners to lift in a smile. She wanted to see that dimple again.

The clank of the backyard gate brought her out of bed, scrambling for her robe.

Please. Please. Please. Don't let it be anything but the wind.

Her heart began to pound faster with each hurried step down the stairway. Surely, it would be days before men from Las Vegas showed up. Every nerve itched like ants beneath her skin. The old sick feeling from eighteen months ago returned in full force.

An outside brightness glimmered through the curtains.

Good. Her motion lights worked. She checked the wall near the garage door. Someone had turned off the security alarm. Or wait...had she remembered to turn it on? How could she make a mistake like that? She couldn't remember. Likely, she'd gotten lax.

Call 911.

Then tell them what? That she received a scary misdialed call from Las Vegas and her motion lights work? Even if Jorge Lazaro, Vincent's old boss, had sent someone, they'd already be inside, convincing her in ways she'd rather not imagine to hand over the information.

So calling the police was out.

She still needed to protect herself as she checked it out. Probably a wild animal caused the light to come on. She glanced up the stairs toward her and her mother's bedrooms and shook her head. No time to waste. Only thing to do was to grab the metal baseball bat from behind the kitchen door and go into the backyard and see what opened the gate.

Yeah, sure.

Many horror movies started with the same premise. *Stupid girl hears noise outside and goes to investigate.* The only difference was she carried a baseball bat and knew how to use it. Vincent had taught her several tricks of his trade.

Who else would go? Her mom? Sending out a sixty-year-old woman made little sense when her daughter was quite capable. In times like these, she really missed having a man around. The image of dark-blue eyes filled with sadness contrasting with a sinful grin and dimple brought her to a halt.

Thinking about Luke would be better saved for another time. She needed to keep her attention on the danger and any thought of asking her neighbor for help had to be forgotten. Probably the wind pushed the gate open.

Leaving the light off in the kitchen, she eased opened the back door and stepped onto the patio with the bat raised high. One step to the side brought her into the shadows. Crickets and tree frogs chirped. Nothing moved. Even the breeze had stopped.

Then she saw him. He charged toward her from the pasture fence. She screamed and swung at the dark form.

"Mary," a deep male voice shouted behind her.

At the same time, arms came around her and jerked the baseball bat out of her hands. Then her mother stepped into the light. *Oh, my God.* She'd almost knocked her mother senseless. On that thought, she spun around, stepping between her mom and whoever had taken the bat.

"Luke?"

He stood a couple of feet away, holding the bat by the wrong end.

"What are you doing out here with my mom?" she asked. He looked dangerous, glaring at her from beneath the lights.

"Lacy wouldn't come when I called and I thought I heard her meowing at the house across the pasture," her mom said before he could answer. "I hurried back home to see if she'd returned." She shivered in the night air, wearing only her cotton pajamas.

Heart in her throat, Mary shook her head. "Mom, Lacy died last year. Remember?"

Her mom wrinkled her forehead and looked around.

Seeing her confusion, Mary knew her mom had experienced another episode. She exhaled and shut her eyes for a second. After taking a few deep breaths, she regained her composure and looked at Luke. He appeared to be studying the older woman closely as most people did after she had done something odd.

Mary turned to grasp her mom's shoulders with a light touch, drawing her attention. "Please go into the bathroom and wash off your feet. I'll be with you in a minute to check on you. Okay?"

It hurt to see the confused look in those eyes she knew so well. Would she ever get used to seeing her mom like this? A woman who'd survived a first husband dying of cancer in his twenties, and stood up against a second husband's abuse. Later, she'd tracked down her teenage daughter to Las Vegas and apologized for not believing her. The same woman who'd cleaned restrooms and mopped floors so her daughter could have decent clothes and a place to stay.

As the screen door clacked behind the older woman, Mary held her hand out to Luke.

Chapter Eight

L uke glanced at her hand and then at the bat, handing it to her small end first. Once Mary clasped it, he thought she looked weary and unsure of what to do with it.

The shadows half hid her face. Her sadness made him wish he could pull her into his arms, to comfort her.

"Alzheimer's or dementia?" When he was younger, he helped his dad during his church visitations with the sick and elderly, so he understood the signs and the difference.

"Alzheimer's. Thank you." She cleared her throat and lowered the bat to her side. The pain in her eyes clearly warned she'd rather talk about anything else. "You kept me from hurting my mom. She's never left the house at night before." Her bathrobe had fallen open, revealing a short cotton gown with small, hot pink flowers that reached just above her knees. Not the sexy negligee he'd always imagined she wore to bed.

The girly gown made her more real. Touchable. His cock took notice too and began to swell in appreciation.

"What are you doing out so late? In my yard?" Her

questions brought him to his senses. He pulled his gaze up to her heavy-lidded eyes.

She glanced away and tugged her robe closed.

Did she think he was a pervert hanging around her house, peeking into the windows? *Of course.* Why should she be any different? Though it went against the grain to explain, he wanted her to think better of him than the rest of Sand City.

"When I can't sleep, I sit on the fence behind the house and stare at the stars." He refused to admit to staring at her house and wondering about her bedroom.

They were alone. For the first time since they'd met, no one to watch their every move.

She appeared relaxed compared to yesterday. He stepped closer. A barely there grin softened her face. The light fragrance of honeysuckle mixed with a fresh breeze engulfed his senses as she drew nearer. He touched her arm. The robe prevented him from feeling her silky skin. He lifted his other hand and touched her cheek. *Yeah. Silky, and oh so soft.*

He shifted from one foot to the other, bringing her within reach. Their bodies brushed against each other. She whimpered, in need, not in protest or disgust. A tilt of his head brought his lips down within a breath of hers. Her body swayed into his. He kissed her, his touch light to assure her all was okay.

She tasted of mint toothpaste and heaven and he wanted more.

He pressed his mouth harder to hers, and her lips parted. Heat tightened his skin and filled his cock as his tongue slid along hers. Desire to taste more of her increased with each thrust of her tongue meeting his.

A vibrating clank exploded behind Luke. They jumped apart. The metal bat rolled off the patio.

"Oh. I forgot I was holding it." Her breathless voice brought a grin to his face.

His kiss had made her forget herself. He liked that. *A sophisticated woman like her lost in a kiss with him. Go figure.*

He wanted to kiss her again. Maybe another time.

"You better go inside and check on your ma," he said gruffly, fisting his hands to resist grabbing her again.

She licked her upper lip. Was she tasting his kiss? Just the thought made him harder.

"You need something better than a bat to protect you," he said as she stooped to pick it up.

Dark round eyes peered up at him. "What? A gun?"

"Yeah." He held out his hand, but she stood without his help.

"Instead of someone taking a bat out of my hands, it would be a gun? Or I could possibly shoot my mom instead of knocking her on the side of the head." She looked at him as if he'd lost his mind for sure.

"I believe you have enough sense to double-check before shooting."

"Maybe so. Doesn't matter. I'll use whatever I feel comfortable with."

"So you played baseball?" He couldn't resist teasing her. Any chance of being alone with her again, teaching her to shoot a gun, tempted him at every turn.

"Softball. You don't have to have a license for that." Her half grin almost pushed him to take a kiss from her once more.

"I'll bring one of mine over for you tomorrow and show

you how to shoot it." He knew of a secluded area in the large pasture near a creek perfect for shooting practice.

"You have guns?" She hugged the bat to her chest.

He'd never been so jealous of an inanimate object in his life.

"I live in the South, don't I?" His drawl stretched the last two words.

"But I thought . . ." She obviously didn't want to finish the sentence. Her deep breath parted the robe enough for him to see the four small buttons down the front. He hadn't noticed them earlier, only one was undone.

"Humph." For some reason, he wanted to be the one to show her how to shoot, and the hell with the consequences. "You want to know, why do I have guns while on parole? Let's say they don't always check, and they're in my dad's name. And like I said, I live in the South."

"Thanks. I'm not sure I'll feel any safer, but, okay, I'll take you up on your offer." On hearing the doubt in her voice, he felt guilty about taking advantage of her fear as an excuse to be around her.

When she turned to go back to the house, he asked, "Why do you feel you need protection? As long as you stay away from the mill on the other end of town, you don't have to worry. People still leave their doors unlocked around here at night and when they go to the store."

A flicker of fear shone in those beautiful eyes as she looked at him.

"Why? Don't you know? It's the South and every God-fearing woman needs to become a proficient shooter. You know to keep varmints out of the backyard," she said in an overdone southern accent.

"Varmints? Right." He stood next to the back door. "I'll wait until you're inside before leaving."

Chuckling, he waited until she closed the door, and he heard a bolt click before heading back to his house. Though she pretended to joke, he'd heard the seriousness in her tone about needing protection. She must know she had nothing to fear from him. Someone had placed a deep-seated fear in her eyes, and he wanted to find out why and then he could take care of whoever it was scaring her.

At least her lie had eased his hard-on.

Chapter Nine

Never an early riser, Mary surprised herself by waking at six-thirty. The smell of frying bacon and worry about her mom pushed her out of bed.

As soon as she reached the kitchen, she grabbed her favorite pink mug and poured a cup of coffee.

"So you woke early too. I expected you to sleep in." Mary leaned a hip against the counter and sipped her drink.

"Why's that?" Without raising her head, her mom stood over the stove, scrambled a couple of eggs and then divided them onto two plates loaded with biscuits and bacon. "Did I wake you? I had some crazy dreams last night. Was I talking to myself?"

"No, no." Mary picked up one plate and sat at the table. She decided it would be best to treat the morning like any other. To make a big deal would only upset both of them.

About thirty minutes later, Luke arrived.

For the rest of the morning and into the afternoon, she kept busy stripping wallpaper in the upstairs master bath and away from where he prepared the family room for painting.

She'd hated lying to him last night. He'd been nothing but nice to her. The call and its heavy silence bothered her to the deep marrow of her bones. Vincent's ex-boss had relished playing cat-and-mouse games with people. The man had a sadistic streak and the money to make it a long game.

Luke had no need to become involved in her problems. He probably had plenty problems of his own. For goodness' sake, Luke had been in prison before and people picked fights with him in the middle of the street. Vincent's ex-boss could create enough trouble to send him back for a much longer time. She needed to keep her mind on taking care of her mom.

If Jorge came, there was no way she could stop him. So last night had been futile in more than one way.

She struggled with pretending nothing else had happened on the patio last night. No kissing. No touching. She fought the memory of his thumb caressing her cheek, the gentleness of his eyes. No matter what she'd heard from the townsfolk, he didn't act crazy or mean. But she'd seen the evidence of his fighting even before Saturday's brawl. The bruises on his face and knuckles. Evidence of a man with a temper. Those types of men she kept at arm's length or further.

She pulled two bags filled with strips of avocado and gold wallpaper downstairs to the kitchen and hesitated when her mom raised a hand for her to stop.

"Mary, go tell that boy to come and eat. I've told him twice and he keeps painting, mumbling something about he didn't need anything." Her mom shook her head. "As tall and skinny as he is, he needs all the food he can get."

Luke had turned down biscuits and ham earlier, claiming he'd already eaten. Now the clock showed one o'clock and all he'd accepted was a sports bottle filled with ice water.

She entered the room and found him working shirtless. Lean muscles glistened with sweat and rippled each time he reached with the roller toward the ceiling. They had opened the windows and turned off the air, providing proper ventilation for the paint fumes. September in Alabama could reach temperatures in the high eighties. Even with a light breeze coming in the windows, the heat and humidity quickly coated the skin.

As he stretched, his loose jeans dropped slightly, showing the edge of hip bones. No underwear? She took a deep breath. The paint fumes caused her to become light-headed and she bumped into a stepladder. Feeling like a clumsy idiot, she almost turned away and returned to the kitchen.

"Hey, I hope you don't mind, but I brought in my fan and turned it on low." He placed the roller in the pan and reached for his shirt.

Then she noticed the bruises and scars across his ribs and stomach. She wanted to ask about them but stopped. Most likely from the last fight along with previous ones. Besides, she needed to keep her distance. Her reaction to his nearness last night was enough of a reason.

No. Bad. Boys. For. Her.

"That's okay. You can crack some windows too." She stared at the floor for a couple of seconds to regain her composure and remember why she'd walked into the room. "Uh, Mom said to stop what you're doing and come and eat lunch or she'll fire you."

One dark brow rose. "She did, eh?"

"No. I just figured that would get you to listen. The

window unit is on in the kitchen. It'll help you cool off. And Mom makes the world's best fried bologna sandwiches."

"Well, I guess I can't turn down the world's best." He smiled and those dark-blue eyes lightened. She'd never seen him smile that big before. Even the dimple became deeper and showed a faint one on the other side of his mouth.

How would he react if she kissed those sexy indentions?

What was she thinking?

She squeezed her eyes shut as he turned—*do not look at his ass*—and walked away. Time to get a hold of herself.

Chapter Ten

His eyes widened as he walked into the kitchen and spotted the plate with two sandwiches and a large helping of potato salad.

"Hope you like potato salad. Mary made it." Mary's mom set a large glass of sweet tea next to the plate.

Luke turned, looking at Mary with brows raised.

"Yes. I really did. Though I have to admit I know only a couple other recipes and nothing else. Mom's the true cook of the family. I've been trying to get her to write them down so I can learn them eventually."

"Yeah, I write them down and she'll no longer need me. She'll put me in an old folks' home." Mrs. Ford's eyes twinkled with her teasing.

"Mom! Stop talking like that. You know better. I plan to dump you at the nearest shopping center." She gave a wicked grin.

He liked their banter. Something he missed with his dad. That was, since his mom's death. Life was unfair. He learned that a long time ago.

They continued to playfully pick on each other. He

even forgot to worry about keeping his elbows off the table. The atmosphere of loving-teasing relaxed his natural guard.

Sooner than he liked, he returned to slapping a paint brush against a dull yellow wall as the women in the other room cleaned.

What would it be like if he owned this farm? If Mary was his woman taking care of her man and their home? He shook his head at his crazy thoughts. Standing on a stepladder was as close to heaven he'd ever get. Dreams were not for people like him.

Chapter Eleven

When Luke finished for the day and her mom settled in front of the TV, Mary drove out to the cemetery.

The narrow paved road wound between stretches of grass and headstones. Sprinkled throughout the cemetery were assorted pots of flowers and statuary. She stopped near a plot with a sleeping stone lamb and a large oak tree.

After her last visit, she'd told her mother she might purchase a stone bench to place beneath the tree. Then she could sit while visiting Vincent.

Her mom had looked so frustrated at her.

"How morbid can you get?" Then she'd hugged her. "Mary, you better stop talking to that stone or people will think you're crazy for sure."

Crazy or not, she found a measure of comfort in talking to Vinny. She kneeled next to the stone etched with Vincent Marcus Hightower. Only the first name was real along with his birth and death dates and the words "Beloved Husband."

"Sorry, Vinny. I followed your written instructions, but

they still found us. I'm not sure what to do next. You said changing our names and using cash as much as possible would cover our tracks, but it took only eighteen months for them to track us down. I'm not good at this. The box you gave me is safe, as you well know. Mom didn't know how important it was when she hid it where she did. I need to pull it from its hiding place. I need the information you died for. I'm sorry." She grabbed the dead flowers she'd left last week and placed them in a plastic sack she'd brought. Then she arranged fresh flowers in the brass planter attached to the marble.

A feeling of helplessness gripped her. Falling to her knees, she knelt in the grass and bowed her head. Thankfully, her tears had dried up months ago. The smell of grass and newly turned soil brought a strange peacefulness to her, but the ache still remained.

"I know I can't give them what they want and expect to live. There has to be another way. Going to the authorities is out. Working with the damn FBI in Vegas sealed your fate. You told me and I wouldn't listen. You did it for me, and I'll never forgive myself. I can't trust any of them. Mom's sick and I never know what she'll blurt out. I can't trust anyone." Thoughts of dark eyes and a goodnight kiss made her whisper, "Maybe one other." She sat on her heels, covered her eyes and groaned.

"You okay, Mary?"

She jerked her head up. Her faced heated with guilt. No way had she conjured up Luke. Yeah, right. A widow thinking of another man, remembering a certain kiss, as she sat by her husband's grave. There was something wrong with that.

"What are you doing here?" she asked. The sinking sun kept his face in silhouette.

He held his hand out and her attention dropped to it. Calluses and blisters attested to how hard he worked. Something about those work-rough hands appealed to her. The way he tenderly held her hand as he pulled her to her feet spoke of his protectiveness. Those hands would be gentle on her skin.

She immediately straightened and released his hand. She swiped at her knees and the seat of her pants as she did her best to hide her blush caused by such wayward thoughts.

As she returned her attention to Luke, she noticed he wore black slacks and a button-down shirt, dressed as if he had a date or planned to go to church. From his off-handed remarks about his father's former profession, she doubted church factored in. That left a date.

But at a cemetery?

Chapter Twelve

"I'm here to visit my ma." He nodded toward the stone lamb.

Luke stuck his hands into his pockets. After being around Mary and Mrs. Ford with their easy mother-daughter relationship, a need to visit his mother's grave pulled him to the cemetery, and he always wore his best clothes out of respect.

When he saw Mary sitting in the grass, head down, he'd sprinted across the cemetery. Unmindful of whose grave he stepped on along the way. He worried she'd fallen and might be bleeding. But she was fine except for a little redness around her beautiful eyes. She'd been crying. His chest tightened at the realization.

With a glance at the headstone, he grimaced when he read the name. When he turned his attention back to her, he caught her staring at the small sleeping lamb.

For more years than he wanted to count, he'd planned to buy his mother a real tombstone, but the cost was beyond his and his dad's means. Something always broke or needed fixing around the farm. Dad claimed she wouldn't care anyway.

"I've wondered who was buried there. The lamb is so pretty." Her soft voice brought him a step closer.

"I picked it out. I was a kid. Figured she would like it too, even if it was only half-priced." Why had he told her that? Time to change the subject.

"Your hand's cold." He lifted it to his cheek and quickly dropped it. What was he doing? "How about a cup of coffee to warm you up?"

He was certifiable. Hadn't he embarrassed her enough? Why would she be seen with him in public?

Her gaze stayed on him for so long, she must be thinking up an excuse to turn him down.

"Never mind." He started to walk on when she touched his arm.

"Sorry. With little sleep last night and all, my brain's working a little slow. I would like that. A cup of coffee, that is."

Surprised but trying not to show it, he nodded. "I'll give you a few minutes to say 'bye while I visit with my ma."

As he walked over to the lamb, he felt her eyes on his back. Did he say something stupid? Damn. With bad girls he knew what to say or do, but with someone like Mary, he stood in a sinking pit of uncertainty. And he constantly made a fool of himself.

"Do you see her, Ma?" he whispered. "Isn't she something? She's a real lady like you."

A breeze blew a strand of hair across his cheek. The sensation reminded him of a finger caressing his face, like the way his mother had touched him as she stood next to his bed at night after reading another chapter of King Arthur.

"Thanks. I knew you'd like her. I wish…" He breathed in deeply.

He glanced over to Mary. She was talking softly again.

Forcing his attention back to his mom's lamb, he shook his head. No matter how many times he apologized to his mother, he knew redemption from his stupid actions that night so many years ago would never be his.

Nevertheless, he murmured, "I'm sorry."

Without another word, Luke stared sightlessly at the lamb. He'd been relieved to know someone else talked to the dead. Maybe they both were crazy. Hell, at least she hadn't run away. He should keep his distance, but he was inexplicably drawn to her.

One wounded soul finding another?

Circumstances beyond their control had pushed them to be people they never expected to become.

He glanced over and caught her staring back. She absent-mindedly pushed back her lovely brunette hair as the wind tossed it around. Before leaving the house, he'd tied his hair at the back of his neck. What did she think of him dressed in his Sunday best?

Without a second thought, he walked toward her with a sureness he hadn't felt in a long time. He'd come to a decision.

As he came nearer, she looked over her shoulder as if expecting someone to be behind her. Why was she nervous? Was she worried about being seen with the town's bad boy? Was she thinking of the gossips in town? Her dead husband? Her mother? He wanted her attention on him and no one else.

"Ready?" Luke held out his hand.

Without hesitation she clasped it and smiled. She squeezed his fingers and returned the pressure, being careful of his strength. Though he barely knew her, he'd do anything for this woman.

<<<>>>

"Let me get this straight. You want me to dig up your husband?" He stared in disbelief at her across the laminated table. Was he to regret his earlier notion? After a quick glance around to confirm no one had heard him, he lowered his head, slowly shaking it side to side. "And they call me crazy."

He should've known something was up when she accepted his offer of coffee. No sane woman would want to be seen with him. Her request doubly proved she was the one crazier.

"Shhh." She leaned nearer. "I know it's a lot to ask and all, but an important box was mistakenly buried with my husband. I didn't worry about it. I thought it would be years, hopefully never, before I would need it."

"Obviously. But how do you mistakenly bury something with a body? And what could be so important to dig up a loved one?"

"The day we moved in, Mom and I talked about placing pictures in the casket before we buried him. It was a sweet tradition Mom had started with her grandparents and I loved the sentimentality of it. In our rush of moving and ensuring Vincent's body arrived here at the funeral home in good order, Mom picked up the wrong box from my dresser drawer. It wasn't until he was buried that I realized the mistake. I'd hoped and prayed the box would never be needed."

Looking at her pale face, he wanted to believe she was telling the truth and she really needed his help. That she wasn't involved in some elaborate plan of Chet Macon's, ex-friend and asshole, to make him break parole by desecrating a grave. If he did this for Mary, he'd give Bubba a big enough reason to put him in jail, if he was caught.

Between Macon and his cousins trying to beat the hell out of him, it could be probable he would try a new tactic. But with Mary. No.

"I'll pay you."

His eyebrows lifted when she named the amount.

"You have that kind of money?"

He thought she was different. But she was like everyone else. They believed he'd do anything for money. He pushed his coffee cup away, sloshing the hot liquid onto the table. Pissed would not cover how he felt.

"For that kind of money, I know at least ten other guys that would be happy to dig up everybody in Sand City Cemetery for you." Shaking his head, he glared at her.

Her eyes widened. "I'm not asking them. I'm asking you. I trust you. And I want only one person dug up." She placed her hand over his.

Trust? That surprised him. Unable to resist, anger shifting to something else, he turned his hand, clasped her chilled one, and pulled her to meet him over the table, almost nose to nose.

"I'll dig up your husband, but not for money."

He stared into her soft brown eyes until understanding washed the color out of her face.

Chapter Thirteen

Mary eased her hand from his, straightening her back as she pulled her dignity around her like a security blanket. He was no different than the other bad men she'd known. Always looking for a way to get into a girl's pants.

Of course, she wanted him. What woman wouldn't? But this was business and she didn't need him in her life. He was trouble with a capital T. She clenched her fingers into fists. She wanted to hit him, but she'd learned men often hit back.

In a voice choked with tears, she whispered, "I thought you were someone I could trust—"

"Is he bothering you, Mrs. Hightower?"

Sheriff Bubba Hagley stopped next to their booth.

The lanky sheriff had introduced himself a couple of weeks after she'd arrived in Sand City. Several times their paths crossed in the diner, when he'd grinned and tipped his hat to her but nothing more. Mostly, he stood at the counter and flirted with Susan.

"No. I just returned from the cemetery. Luke and I were remembering those we lost."

She'd lied without missing a beat. Old habits were hard to break. For some reason, the bright smile and crisp uniform of Sheriff Hagley set off alarms in Mary's head. He looked too clean-cut to be real. Like he was playing a part to impress the townsfolk.

"That's mighty kind of you, Luke ol' boy."

Bubba's words and tone sounded like what a friend would say to another. Yet the usual hum of conversations and the clicking of silverware scraping plates and glasses being loaded into busboy tubs came to a grinding halt. As if everyone expected Luke to explode into a murderous rage.

Luke ignored the sheriff by pulling out paper napkins from the metal dispenser and wiping up spilled coffee. She'd heard they were friends once. Now he treated the sheriff as if he was nothing more than a fly buzzing around his head.

The sheriff remained standing as if he had more to say.

What was the sheriff waiting for? Luke tossed the wadded napkin into the cup. Then he leaned forward and grabbed her hand.

"I accept your offer," he said in a suggestive tone.

She fought the urge to snatch her hand back and glanced at Bubba's face. What was Luke up to? The sheriff would have no idea of what she offered. Oh, goodness. He would think....

Unable to resist any longer, she took a peek at the sheriff's face. His light-blue eyes looked at her in manly speculation.

She was stuck. No way could she tell the sheriff the real offer. Men. Her cheeks heated. How many years had it been since she'd blushed this much? Years, until she met Luke.

"I'll leave you two alone. You're a lucky fellow."

The sheriff chuckled as he walked to the takeout counter and Susan.

Mary jerked her hand out of Luke's grasp.

"That was hateful," she whispered.

"He believed you were asking me out," Luke said with a smirk.

"No. You know what I mean. You expect more than a date for helping me."

She caught the flash of amusement in his navy-blues. He was laughing at her. Sex wasn't a laughing matter.

"What's so funny?" She wanted to slap that smug face. When had she become so savage?

"You, thinking I'll ask for your delicious body in trade." He reclaimed her hand, squeezing when she tried to jerk away. "When we make love, it will be because we both want it. Not because we owe the other anything. On equal ground you could say."

Warmth swept down her spine. His confidence and touch caused her body to soften.

No. No. No.

No sex with a bad boy. She swallowed and took a deep breath, then gave him a half grin. Friends. They could be friends. Yeah, right. The way he touched her hand—his fingers caressing hers—and his voice deep, soothing to her strung-out nerves. No friend had ever made her feel so special. Not counting the kiss last night.

Quit thinking about it.

He was driving her totally loony.

"Then what did you mean by not for money?" she asked.

He flipped her hand over and traced the lines on her palm. *Oh, that feels so good.*

"One date." His dimple showed up.

Perversely, she was disappointed. What was wrong with her?

Being wishy-washy was not her usual way of handling her feelings about men. When she had met Vinny, she'd known he was the one for her. They had slept together that first night and he'd shown her how a man made love. But she knew he was the type of guy who never had to work at getting a woman to do what he wanted and that included her.

One of the benefits of being older, she had more self-control. But at that moment, she was beginning to doubt her conviction.

Luke's scrutiny warned her he planned to make her scream his name numerous times. If that wasn't enough, his husky whispers shot tremors from her breasts to between her legs. It took all of her power not to grab his hand and rush out of the diner to the nearest bed.

Okay. There was a little of the bad girl left in her. Staying on the straight and narrow was difficult, and having such a dark, dangerous man looking at her as if she spun gold was wonderful.

Going back and forth in wanting him and telling herself she shouldn't was almost as nerve-racking as knowing Jorge Lazaro wanted to break both of her legs or worse. Probably worse.

A callused finger moved to the back of her hand and traced the delicate veins. The air in the diner became heavy. She took a long, deep breath. His touch felt so good. It'd been way too long.

"I couldn't resist teasing you. Have dinner with me.

That's all I want. I can wait until you really trust me enough with your secrets, like why you want that box."

Hooded navy-blue eyes, scruff on his face, dark hair softly curling over his ears and cupping his jaw, he portrayed the picture-perfect bad boy. Why bad boys? Why? Those masculine lips saying such wonderful things to her were made for kissing. Full lower lip and a small dip on the upper one, she wondered if they tasted as good as they appeared. She remembered how gentle he'd been as he kissed her and afterwards but not much more.

"Okay. It's a deal," she said breathlessly.

His devilish grin woke her from a lust-filled trance. She'd almost forgotten the real reason they agreed on dinner. Digging up the past.

Literally.

<<<>>>

Mary remained seated in the diner as Luke walked out. He had a few ideas on how to open the grave. He'd warned her it would be a few days before he could arrange something. The simple task of pulling out the box her mother had placed there had grown complex.

What a joke. Vincent had tried to guarantee a new life for her, and there she was about to break a half dozen laws.

How in the world were they going to lift a cement vault lid that probably weighed hundreds of pounds? That was if they dug down to it before someone called the authorities. To add to the problem, Vincent was buried near Main

Street. Anybody could drive by and see what was happening.

"Mary? Are you okay?" Susan sat in Luke's spot, pushing a cup of coffee toward her.

"Thanks." Mary took a sip. Perfect with a little sugar and milk. "I'm fine. Just tired I guess. Mom had a bad night last night and kept me up a little late."

They sat for a few seconds drinking their coffee. Mary liked Susan. Mainly because the woman's humor matched her own. A little off-kilter and never truly mean-spirited.

Mary had come to know her friend well. When Susan cleared her throat and pursed her lips, she had something to say Mary wouldn't like.

"Living in a wild town like Las Vegas, you probably know more about life and people than I ever will." Susan patted her hand. "Oh, blast, how can I say this." She searched the ceiling for an answer until returning her gaze to Mary's. "Luke is nothing but trouble. His temper is legendary. His mother was out of the loony bin only a couple months when she died. Rumors say he had something to do with that. I can't with good conscience let you be fooled by his caring act."

Mary squeezed her hand in appreciation. "Thank you for worrying about me. Luke and I are friends and that's all. He's working as the handyman at my farm and nothing more." It was basically the truth.

Mary kept her grin steady as a way to reassure Susan all was okay. Luke would do this one favor, and they would go on a date as payment. It didn't mean they would sleep together.

Who was she trying to convince? Susan or herself? Just because she wondered if the kiss was as mind-blowing as she remembered, didn't mean she was going to kiss him again. Did it? The only reason he would risk breaking parole was that he probably felt sorry for her, probably thought she was lonely for some male companionship. That was all. At the same time, the nagging voice in her head taunted her with a clear, drawn out, "Sure."

"Sorry. I guess when I saw you and Luke walking in together, I couldn't help worrying. He's had two fights this week with Chet and his cousins, besides the one you saw Saturday."

"I understand your concern. I happened to be at the cemetery at the same time he was. His mom is buried just a few feet from Vincent." She bit her lip. Susan was on her mom's side about Mary's frequent visits to the cemetery.

"You know when I told you last week that you needed to move on, I didn't mean with Luke."

Mary fought a giggle. There wasn't anything funny about the situation. Maybe the whole mess had gotten to her. Certainly she had a reason to be stressed. Vincent's Vegas employer wanted her dead and she planned for an ex-con to help her dig up her husband. In doing all of this, they'd break several laws and her friend was worried about who she might date. Men like Luke were nothing but trouble, but would a good ol' boy do this for her?

"Don't worry. We're just friends. That's all." Before Susan could comment on Mary's unconvincing denial, her brother hollered from the kitchen something about her chocolate pies.

To think on it, it was funny that Susan acted as if she'd never lived anywhere but Sand City. True, she'd been born here, though her family left when she was ten. After her training with some famous chef in New York, she returned home a couple of years ago to help her brother.

"We'll talk again later." Susan scooted out of their

booth, waving her hands frantically at Bill. "I'm coming, I'm coming! You better not have burnt my pies!"

Relieved to escape any more questions, Mary headed toward the exit as Susan ran into the kitchen.

<<<>>>

After a second day of painting, Luke had asked Mary if she still wanted to learn how to shoot a gun. Deep inside she knew she should say no. Common sense told her she really didn't need lessons or to be around him any more than necessary.

When had she ever let common sense rule her?

Though she could see the back of his house from across the pasture, she'd never been up the long dirt drive. The rose bushes along the fence running up to the house appeared well-kept and full of heavy blooms of red, pink, and yellow. On the house, white siding with deep-blue shutters invited everyone inside. A large patchwork of Sweet Williams and marigolds bloomed on each side of the steps. Four wooden rockers looked inviting lined along one end of the porch, lightly rocking in the early fall breeze.

Before she had a chance to knock, Reverend Blackwood opened the front door.

"Hello, Mrs. Hightower. I'm Luke's dad."

"Please call me Mary."

"A good biblical name." He stepped to the side. "Call me Zeke."

"Thank you, Zeke." She walked into the foyer with his silent invitation and grinned. It was easy to see why his church mourned his retirement. Personable and quick to put a stranger at ease, Luke's father stood almost a foot taller, yet didn't tower over her in an attempt to intimidate like many large men.

"Would you like a glass of tea? Some cookies?"

The Southern way of always asking a guest if they were thirsty or hungry still enchanted Mary.

"No, thank you. Luke and I need to get moving before dark."

He nodded to the couch and she took a seat.

"Yeah. He's taking you out to the north forty. That acreage is so far out, any stray bullets should hit only trees or dirt." Zeke groaned as he sank into a brown leather recliner. "Excuse me. My old bones creak and ache at the end of the day."

Unsure of what to say, she was surprised that Luke would tell his dad about their practice. An activity that could put him back into prison.

She looked around the small den. It was obvious a woman hadn't lived in the house for many years. Though the outside boasted flowers by the armloads, the inside was spartan in comparison. Only the large, multicolor, hand-woven rug brightened the room and gave it a lived-in feel.

Zeke picked up a remote and turned off the television. That was when she heard water running in a shower. Then the noise stopped.

"Luke will be ready soon. Sally gave him a hard time today." He chuckled.

Her eyebrows lifted in question at his comment. Luke hadn't said anything about a girlfriend. When he kissed her last night, he hadn't acted as if someone else was in his life. Then again, she'd been trying to convince herself the kiss meant nothing. She'd gone almost two years without someone to hold her at night, kiss her as a desirable woman.

Now was not the time to start feeling sorry for herself. She needed to stay alert and stop anyone from hurting her mom or taking away the new life she'd planned.

"Sorry for being late. It'll only take me a minute and we can get going," Luke said.

Mary looked at Luke. He stood in the doorway leading to a dark hall. Dressed in low-riding jeans and no shirt, he rubbed a towel across his wet hair. She swallowed her sigh. The ripped abs and well-toned pectorals made her appreciate being a woman. Remembering the reverend was in the room, Mary tried to look anywhere but at the mouth-watering bad boy. Even his bruises were fading a little. Unable to resist, her gaze returned to his retreating figure.

"Oh, my God! What happened?"

On his back toward one side was a half-moon bruise about the size of her open palm. Was that from the fight?

He twisted and covered the black-and-blue mark with his hand.

"Sally. She nipped at me. She gets a little mad when you clean her hooves and I had my mind on other things and didn't move out of the way in time." He shot her a grin before walking away.

Hooves?

"Oh, the blind mare," she said as she slumped back on the couch. Silly for her to worry. Luke didn't belong to her, especially as she kept wavering on how she should treat him. A friend one moment and desired lover the next. Maybe they could be friends with benefits.

She silently sighed. Why couldn't she rein in her libido?

Within moments, Luke sauntered back in, buttoning up a denim shirt that brought out the blue in his eyes.

He wasn't making it easy on her. Eyes sparkling with mischief, a grin that was an odd mixture of shyness and boldness, and his hair, a little long and still damp, sticking up in a charming, boyish way. Her hand itched to smooth it down and run her fingers through the damp strands. He looked delicious enough to eat.

After waving goodbye to his dad, she hopped into his truck—oddly, clean and clean smelling, no cigarette or illegal substance odor—and he shifted gears to head down a dirt road not far from his house. She was excited. It had been years since she'd been alone with a man who wasn't her husband.

Her attention became glued to his large hands holding the steering wheel. Would he hold her while they were alone? Tingling scattered across her skin. Maybe kiss again? Would she let him? Probably, despite her better judgment. Crap. She crossed her arms, hoping he wouldn't see her erect nipples jutting beneath her blouse. What would he do or say if he did?

Chapter Fourteen

The short trip brought them near a small stream and an old wooden fence. As soon as they stopped, Luke lifted a bulging plastic bag from the truck bed. At the fence, he pulled out several cans and bottles and lined them up along the top rail.

He returned and stopped beside her. When he pulled out a gun from the waistband of his jeans, he lifted her hand and folded her fingers around the grip. "This is a Smith and Wesson revolver. Its handle is small enough for a woman to hold and light enough to keep in your purse. Place your hand slightly lower over the other and let your index finger rest lightly beneath the trigger. Don't put your finger on the trigger until you're ready to shoot."

Luke stepped a little closer to her. Of course, all in the name of teaching her how to hold the gun. What harm would there be if his hip brushed hers? She smelled so sweet. His gut clenched when she shifted to look down the barrel at one of the targets and her hip brushed him. Agony. His concentration wavered as he worked at not grinding himself against her.

She fired, the pistol jerked up, and thankfully he had his hand over hers. He caught the pistol as she released it.

"That was louder than I expected. Sorry." She laughed, eyes glittering in the evening light. "I hate acting like a wimp."

"No. You're not a wimp. This gun is probably too powerful for you to handle. Let me help you. Don't pull on the trigger until I tell you." At least the shot brought him back to his senses. He needed to concentrate on the lessons and not on her delectable body.

"I think this will do. If you get it any smaller it would be a derringer. One or two shots would not keep me safe enough."

He raised his eyebrows at that.

"So you know about guns?"

"A little. My husband carried one."

"Was he in law enforcement?

"No."

She didn't say more and he got the feeling she'd rather change the subject. So he returned to giving her instructions and a few pointers. When she shot the revolver several more times and hit a whole row, he decided it was enough.

"I haven't lost my touch," she said excitedly.

She handed the pistol back and wrapped her arms around his neck.

He struggled to push the safety on as her firm breasts pressed into his torso. Damn. The woman was going to be the death of him. He'd made a promise to enjoy her company and no more. But a parolee had no business messing with a fine, upstanding woman like her. Ironic, since he was handling a gun.

"Yo! Lu! What's up? Do you have to hold a gun on a girl to get her to hug ya?" Evil slammed his truck door shut.

Luke hadn't heard the old Toyota pickup pull in beside his clunker. Considering Evil's pickup needed a new muffler, it told him how much his attention centered on Mary.

When Mary dropped her arms and stepped to the side, he almost punched Evil in his smirky face. He wanted her clinging to him again.

"What do you want?" Luke glanced at his friend.

To keep from indulging in his impulse to see Evil on the ground bleeding, Luke turned, unloaded the pistol, and then placed it inside the padded metal case.

"I couldn't believe what your dad told me. How stupid can you be to break parole like that? Out here shooting guns, showing off in front of your new pus—"

When he came to his senses, he was on top of Evil, pounding his face, and Mary was beating his back with her fists as she screamed for him to stop.

"Stop it! It's not worth getting thrown into prison again. I've been called worse." She pulled on his arm.

He looked at her and realized she was scared, wide-eyed and pale. Releasing Evil, he stood up. Seeing her afraid because of something he did was like having a bucket of ice thrown in his face. Never would he want her frightened of him. Hell, he'd done it good now.

"Sorry, man, I overreacted." Luke still wanted to pulverize Evil's face. "Don't ever talk about Mary like that again." He reached out a hand to help the man up.

Evil stared back, blood streaming from his nose and mouth. One eye was swollen and quickly turning blue beneath it. He would be sporting a black eye for a few days.

"You're right for taking up for your lady. I deserved it." He grasped Luke's hand and stood, slapping at the dirt on his T-shirt and jeans. Then he swung.

Stars burst from Luke's skull and bells tolled in the distance. Evil sure had a nasty left. The ground met his back with a hollow thump. Between Evil and Sally, his back would be sore as hell for days on end.

"Stop! Both of you. This isn't solving anything." Mary kicked Evil. "Stupid male pride."

"Damn! Take it easy. For a woman wearing tennis shoes you got a mean kick." Evil stumbled back, rubbing his shin. "Hey, man. I think she likes you. She got all protective over your ass."

Luke chuckled. He liked having Mary take up for him. He tenderly touched the corner of his mouth, tasting blood from where his teeth met his cheek.

"Hey, Mary, if you don't mind, take the sack and gather up the targets." Luke nodded to the bag hanging on a post.

That should give Evil some time to say whatever he came to tell him. Luke stood and then walked over to his truck. Leaning back against the front grill, he waited for Evil to limp over to him.

"What made you come out here? Surely it wasn't to find someone to beat your ass."

Evil shook his leg as if to shake off the pain. "I saw an old friend of yours last night in Birmingham."

"Who?"

"Woodrow Beacon."

"Hmm."

Luke had met the man while in prison. Most of the inmates called him Big Daddy. A big, rotund fellow with a look and manner that misled more than one convict into believing he was a pushover. When he wasn't in jail for beating one of his girls, he ran a prostitute ring near the Birmingham International Airport. Besides keeping his whores in line, he was a good contact when you needed a plugger. An assassin.

"He said to tell you that a fellow from Las Vegas has been asking about your lady."

Luke glanced over to where Mary was searching near some tall grass for the cans she'd managed to hit. "How does he know about Mary?"

"I mentioned you were hung up on someone new in town and probably wouldn't meet us. He said someone had been asking about a woman that had recently moved to Sand City. The description matched."

The concerned look on Evil's face made Luke wary. "You're not telling me something."

The dark-haired man shifted his weight and stepped a little closer. "He said her name was Mary Hayden and her stage name was Honey," he said in a low voice.

"Stage name?"

"She's an ex-showgirl. He worked as an enforcer for Jorge Lazaro. Lazaro owns a couple small casinos in Las Vegas and Atlantic City. She was in the lineup at his casino in Vegas. That's how her husband met her. After they'd been married for a while, her husband decided to get out of the business but it was too late. His body was blown into big chunks by a car explosion. That was eighteen months ago. The word on the street is she's blackmailing Lazaro to leave her alone. And he's getting nervous about the information she's holding."

Before Luke could ask anything more, Mary walked up and handed him the stuffed bag. "Are you two okay now?"

The curious look Evil gave Mary had Luke wanting to mash in his face again. Her oblivious attitude told him Mary was used to lewd stares from men. Why hadn't he noticed it before? Maybe because whenever he stared at her she blushed. He'd never noticed her blushing for any other man and plenty had looked at her long and hard in Sand City.

"Mary, this is Evil. Ignore him. He's an asshole and doesn't know any better."

"Evil, huh? I can't imagine your momma would name you Evil."

"No, ma'am. She named me John Thomas. I'm known to pull a prank or two on my friends. So I got stuck with the nickname."

Chapter Fifteen

ary guessed Evil never stayed in trouble with a woman long considering his sexy grin and good looks. What woman could resist? That was, besides her. Luke's soft-spoken manner and unassuming ways were more her type.

Oh, goodness, he was her type. Wasn't that why she was struggling with her attraction? She rolled her eyes and returned her attention to what was being said.

Evil glanced at Luke. "I guess I'll leave you two alone. It's about to get dark anyway and out here in the boondocks the nights get as cold as a witch's..." He looked at Mary. "Huh, it gets mighty cold. Well, I better get back before Smooth gets all bent out of shape about me being late for dinner and eats all my pizza."

As Evil drove away, she tilted her head, trying to figure out Luke's friend. "Is Smooth his wife?"

"Wife?" When she nodded, he laughed and kept laughing until his face turned red. "Hell, no! Smooth's his brother. They argue all the time about who eats the most and who's the worst cook."

She liked how his smile made his eyes twinkle like stars in a twilight sky. He continued to grin as they stared at each other.

The tree frogs began to chirp and a slight breeze off the nearby pond brought chill bumps to her arms. Rubbing her arms against the cold, she was drawn by the slow change of light amusement to heavy interest on his face. The shadows leached the softness from his features, giving him a dangerous appearance.

"I guess I need to get home and check on Mom." She hoped to break the spell he'd cast with his intense stare. It wasn't enough. She remained enthralled.

"Who called you worse?"

"Pardon?"

"You said you'd been called worse. Who was the asshole? Was it your husband?"

That finally got her attention.

"Vincent? No." She shook her head. "He had his faults but talking ugly to me wasn't one of them." Her gaze drifted over to the truck, wishing they could skip this part. She'd hoped to hold off this conversation for a few more weeks. "I guess you haven't heard the gossip." She waited for his nod. "I was a professional dancer. A showgirl."

"A showgirl, huh?"

"Yeah."

Most men's gazes would drop to her breasts and some-times further as they imagined her in a skimpy costume. His stayed on her face.

"So who called you worse?"

The anger vibrating from him didn't bother her. She could tell the negative emotion was directed at the unknown asshole. "Don't worry. It was a long time ago before I met my husband. No one dared insult me after it was known that I was married to Vincent."

"Why's that?" Shoulders stiff and hands fisted at his sides, he looked as if he expected a blow.

Only her mother knew the truth about how Vincent had made a living. Mary dismissed the thought of lying. It was all part of turning that new leaf she kept twisting and misusing in an effort to be a good girl. Life had never been black and white. It was all about the gray. Heavens. She wasn't sure if she knew how to be good. She only knew what felt right.

"Vincent worked for Jorge Lazaro. Lazaro owns a lot of property that includes casinos. He isn't a nice man. My husband took care of problems that crept up."

When they dated, she'd been ignorant of his job. In fact, it wasn't until they were married eight months that she finally understood the violence her husband was capable of. She'd always wondered how long it would have been before she put together the clues: spots of blood on his shirts, numerous guns and knives, unexplained bruises on his knuckles. If she hadn't forgotten her cell phone in Vincent's office, how long would she have stayed ignorant? The massive suite was located in the basement of the casino. Through the door she heard sounds like someone exercising, using a punching bag. Only when she opened the door, Vincent was punching a man in the kidneys as the guy's body hung from the ceiling.

She blinked slowly to erase the image from her mind.

"What's in the box, Honey?"

"I really...how did...Evil told you. What did he tell you?"

"He told me Lazaro is looking for you. That you have something he wants. What's in the box?"

He looked at her differently now. A knot formed in her throat. She knew how many people thought the girls that performed in such shows were only whores. They were unaware many had families, went to PTA meetings, drove minivans and took kids to ball games. Normal lives. As normal as could be when they worked until two in the morning, and if they were lucky, slept until noon. "Honey was my stage name."

"Would you rather I call you Mary Hayden?" His face revealed nothing.

Her knees began to tremble. She stumbled to the truck and placed her hand on the hood to remain on her feet.

"There's no legal way you could've found that out." She shook her head. "I'd rather you call me Mary Hightower."

"I like Honey. It suits you." One step brought him closer. He slid the back of one finger down her cheek. She turned her head from his touch.

"That's not who I am now. Please. What else did he say?" she whispered.

"That you're blackmailing a very dangerous man. Your husband's former boss." His body almost touched hers. Anger radiated off each lean solid inch of his body. "What's in the box, Mary?"

"I don't know."

"Why don't I believe you?"

Heat flushed her face. She released the anger building inside.

"Well, isn't that too bad." She grabbed the front of his shirt. "Haven't you ever been afraid? Maybe I thought of it as a Pandora's box. Something you're safer not knowing what's inside. The contents could kill you or those you love. I know it killed Vinny."

Chapter Sixteen

The mood in the truck during the short drive back to his house where she'd left her car was strained. Only the sound of the wind hitting the windows sliced through the silence.

Mary pulled at her blouse and then wiped her sweaty palms on her jeans. Her fidgeting bothered him. He shouldn't have let his temper get away from him. She'd only lied because in her mind she needed to protect herself and her mother.

When she began to fuss with her hair, Luke grabbed her hand and held it between them.

"Don't worry. I won't tell anyone," he said.

"What do you want in return?"

He glanced at her. He should be insulted, but he had an idea of the kind of people she came in contact with, considering her husband likely worked in a crime organization. Again, she was probably thinking he wanted her body in exchange for his cooperation to keep his mouth shut. Even in the dashboard lights, he could see the worry lines on her forehead.

"Once more, I expect nothing. If I did, I wouldn't want anything you're not willing to give," he said, the words firm and gentle, hoping his tone reassured her he would protect her, look out for her. That he was the right guy to trust.

"Okay." She sighed.

"I came up with an idea of how we can get the box." The look she gave him would make up for all the favors he'd have to call in. He liked thinking he was someone's hero.

"How?"

"Mr. Houghton died this morning, and I've been told, his plot is over the hill from your husband's. But your husband's grave will be dug up by mistake. I figure with a little inventiveness I can use the backhoe to open the vault and the coffin and do it quickly. I'll have about thirty minutes before anyone notices and if I'm lucky another thirty to close it up."

"Do you really believe no one will stop you?"

"Most people who pass a cemetery have no reason to question whether or not someone is digging in the right spot."

"True. What can I do to help?"

He'd never been squeamish about many things but digging up a body was definitely at the top of the list. In prison he learned a lot of strange things and what happened to a body in a sealed vault was one of them. No way would he let her near her husband's coffin.

"Nothing. Just wait to hear from me. They normally dig at daybreak. Most people are still having breakfast before leaving for work."

He pulled the truck next to her car. A light flickered in the front window of the house. His dad was watching television. The front porch light was on.

Staring at each other, neither wanted to make the first

move to leave. He struggled to think of an excuse for her to come inside. He liked that she enjoyed his company as much as he did hers and hoped she would talk more about her past. She appeared to not be upset with him anymore.

"I guess I'll see you tomorrow then." She reached for the latch handle but stopped. "I can't thank you enough. A dinner out just doesn't seem enough."

"Why, Ms. Hightower, what are you offering?"

When she gasped, he started laughing. For a woman who had lived in a city steeped with sexuality, and his imagination of how skimpy her costumes had been during the shows with hundreds of men watching, she was so easy to fluster.

"I didn't mean...I was just saying..." He watched her chest heave as she tried to calm herself. Something about a woman who had such control. His type of woman. "How about dinner Friday night?" Her half grin and assertiveness were hot as hell.

"First, let's see if my idea works."

She nodded and slipped out and walked to her car.

Mentally patting himself on the back for not taking advantage of her, he stood on his front porch until she drove away.

Chapter Seventeen

She'd been dreading, but expecting another call which finally happened two days later. When the phone rang, she scrambled for it before her mother heard in the shower. She fumbled and it danced in the air and luckily she caught it. Crap, her nerves were shot.

"Hello," her voice squeaked.

"Hello, Honey, it's been a long time."

"Jorge." She closed her eyes, glad she'd regained control of her voice and fingers.

The chuckle was as malicious as its owner. Memory of how he'd looked the last time she'd seen him caused her stomach to roll in disgust. Despite slicked-down hair, manicured nails, and a lewd stare, he was a handsome man. Most women sighed over his looks. To her, he looked like the typical slimy, two-bit mobster from any B-rated crime movie.

Anyway, like her mother always said, "Pretty is as pretty does."

So in Mary's eyes, he was ugly as homemade sin.

"You've got something of mine."

"Don't make me use it," she said.

She never was good at bluffing. Vinny had always told her to stick with the slots. Poker was for those good at lying. It was no surprise Jorge was known as a successful, high-stakes poker player.

The nasty chuckling crawled out of the phone.

"Now, Honey, you know better than to threaten me. I don't take threats lightly. I do have to say you gave me a good run for my money. Took me a little longer to find you than I had expected." She heard someone talking in the background and Jorge placed his hand over the mouthpiece for a few seconds. She heard Jorge's muffled voice and then a female's. He returned with a threat to Mary. "I heard those old farm houses can go up like kindling. By the way, how's your mom? Loony as ever?"

"Vincent said if you tried touching me or my mom to turn in the evidence to the authorities and you'll go away for a long time."

"You don't want to do that. I can promise you, if I ever see the police knock on my door, you won't live to see me go to trial. Who would take care of that little old lady then?"

Mary slumped into the chair next to the phone.

"Honey, did you understand what I said?"

"Yes," she whispered.

"You be a good girl and this Sunday I'll meet you by Vincent's grave at eight p.m. You bring the evidence he gave you or I'll make sure you and your mom wished you died with that two-faced husband of yours."

"No. I'll meet you at Bill's Diner in the center of Sand City. I don't trust you. I want plenty of people around."

"Sure. I'll find it. Such a little hick town should be easy to get around in. Hate to see Vincent's body turn over in his casket anyway. That is, whatever was left of him."

Mary slammed the phone down on his grating laugh.

She knew there was no way Jorge would let her live after she gave him the evidence. What could she do? Trust Jorge to keep his word or go to the police with the evidence.

If she notified the police, as slow as justice moved, Jorge would arrange her death before his appeals ran out. Her other choice was to run again and work at covering her tracks better.

She placed her elbows on the table and held her head in despair. None were options that would improve her life span.

So far all she'd proven was that she wasn't good at running or threatening.

<<<>>>

Mary's head tossed back and forth on her pillow. The dream refused to release her from its silky choking threads.

She didn't want to relive that night. The night she lost Vinny. It had been almost a month since the last time she had the nightmare.

In the out-of-focus way of dreams, she sat at the dining room table, furious he'd forgotten to call and warn her of being late.

The doorbell chimed. She swallowed deeply and stared wide-eyed at the door for a split second. Something had gone terribly wrong.

Don't open the door.

It was to be a simple meeting with his FBI contact in the middle of the desert. Like innocent children, they'd believed they would be safe from prying eyes. Miles of cacti and sagebrush, no one could sneak up and hear their conversation.

Each thundering step drew her closer to the front door. The door grew and grew until she felt like Alice in Wonderland after she tried her "Drink Me" bottle. Each step slowed until she moved in a macabre dance. Her small hands twisted the huge knob and there stood Vincent. Burnt and bloody from the explosion that had taken his life, he stared at her with unseeing, lidless eyes.

She woke screaming. Covering her mouth with a trembling hand, she stifled the sound, hoping she hadn't awakened her mother. The clock on her nightstand read two-twenty-two in the morning.

The house was quiet. Thankfully her mom slept on.

Since his death, her mom had tried talking her into seeing a psychotherapist, but Mary knew what the doctor would say. That she missed her husband and felt guilty about pushing Vincent into turning against his boss. Oh, she missed her husband so much, but she knew even if she hadn't asked him to stop, his violent death was inevitable. She'd always heard a violent life led to a violent death. So true for Vinny.

They hadn't counted on Jorge Lazaro planting a bug on his own enforcer's sedan. Somehow Jorge had already guessed Vincent would turn state's evidence and planned his right-hand man's death. By simply dialing from a burner phone to the SIM card hidden beneath the bumper of Vincent's car, Jorge could hear any conversation within thirty meters.

Once the police had found the charred SIM card and had asked her about it and explained what it was used for, she was able to piece the story together. Vinny had told her many times, Jorge was a sneaky and distrustful SOB. His favorite method of taking out the competition was an explosive beneath a car. Why hadn't Vinny suspected his boss would do the same to his? She would never know.

Tomorrow... She squeezed her eyes shut for a moment... This morning, Luke had expected to retrieve the box for her. Mr. Houghton's funeral had been delayed until Thursday, while waiting for out-of-state mourners. Why she trusted a known criminal to bring her evidence that could mean life or death, she wasn't sure, but who else besides her mom could she count on?

Surely the dream returned only because Jorge had called. She'd be okay. She would think of something. For now, she'd keep the call to herself. There wasn't anything Luke could do to help besides what he now was planning.

She checked the newly installed security system. All the correct lights were on green. So all should be working. All she needed to do when she left the house was to press a button, and they would turn to red, arming the system. Keeping her and her mom safe. But she knew better. She knew trusting something so easily manipulated meant trouble.

It was nearly nine o'clock that morning when Luke showed up in the backseat of Sheriff Bubba Hagley's marked SUV.

Ready to fall to the ground in a heap of nerves, she forced her legs to move and stepped out onto the porch after shutting down the alarm. Had Luke betrayed her? She would take whatever consequences dished out by the sheriff. Taking one day at a time had become her motto the past eighteen months.

The sheriff walked around and opened the back passenger's door. Luke stood, slapped at his jeans, causing clouds of dust to billow in the air. No handcuffs. That was a good sign.

"Mrs. Hightower, Luke claims he's working for you and your mom as a handyman," Bubba said.

Remain calm. He'd said handyman not grave robber.

"Yes. He is."

She looked at Luke. His red-clay-encrusted denim jacket and jeans appeared stiff and uncomfortable. When he raised his head, she gasped. One eye was nearly closed and the cut on his cheek seeped blood.

"Oh, my God, Luke. What happened?"

She barely refrained from touching him. Employer wouldn't hug an employee.

"Don't worry, ma'am. Good thing he was driving by when he noticed where the backhoe had been left unattended and how Trim Posey had dug in the wrong place. Actually, he dug up your husband's grave."

"My husband?" Her voice steady, she kept her gaze on Luke.

"Yes, ma'am. Luke was filling the hole in when Trim jumped him. Ol' Trim's never been quite right and when he's drinking he can do crazy things. I've got him in the jail until he sobers up."

When Luke jerked his head toward Bubba she knew they needed to be alone. Did he get the box?

"I see. Thank you, Sheriff, for letting me know." She reached for Luke's arm. "And thank you for putting my husband's grave to rights. Let's check out that cut and get you cleaned up."

She hoped the sheriff would leave as she turned to walk with Luke into the house. The thump of a boot landing on the bottom step behind them warned her she wasn't going to be so lucky.

As soon as they walked into the living room, she reached for Luke's jacket. "Let me help you out of that."

"No." He caught her hands and shook his head.

"Luke, don't be rude. You're getting dirt all over the lady's floor," said Bubba, checking out the room as if he expected mementos from her past life.

"That's okay. We can go into the kitchen. Easier to clean up in there." She'd started down the short hallway when she heard the scuffle behind her.

She turned to see Bubba struggling with Luke and his jacket. "Come on. Get the jacket off," insisted the sheriff. Luke fought one-handed as his other held the small of his back. A flash of maple wood caught her attention. He got it.

Then everyone came to a standstill when the wooden box—the size that could hold several thick love letters or folded papers—crashed to the floor. The lid came off and a small white teddy bear holding a red heart with a key hanging from its neck rolled out and landed next to the sheriff's foot.

Mary and Luke froze as Bubba picked up the box and teddy bear. She'd never opened the box after Vincent had given it to her, so she was as surprised as everyone. What had happened to the evidence?

The sheriff looked at Luke in confusion.

"The Hightowers were nice to give me a job and it was a surprise thank you." His jaw set, he looked to be a man embarrassed by the gesture.

"Sorry, man. I didn't know you had a present for Mrs. Hightower." The sheriff placed the teddy bear back into the box and handed it over to Luke. "Sorry to ruin the surprise. I guess I'll head out now. Sorry again."

Red-faced, Bubba scrambled across the living room.

The clacking of the screen door assured her the coast was clear.

"Are you okay?"

"Yeah. Nothing I did got rid of Bubba and then he insisted on taking me to work. My truck wouldn't start. Hicks's Auto is working on it. I think Bubba just wanted an excuse to come here."

Luke walked over to the kitchen sink, setting the box with the bear inside on the counter, and washed his hands.

She handed him a towel. "He's not like any sheriff I've ever met."

"Yeah. I guess so. He's almost as nosey as those two old hens that hang out at Bill's Diner. Can't even cut grass without one of them ogling me from behind their curtains." Luke shook his head.

On remembering what the women had said last weekend, she tried her best to hold back a giggle. When he looked as if he wanted to choke her, she burst out laughing. Really it wasn't that funny, but she figured with her nerves drawn tight, worrying what the sheriff would discover or say, and the thought of those two dirty-minded, old women peeking at hot, shirtless Luke, like their friend Ruth, there was no way she could hold back. It was so much better than crying.

"Are you laughing at me, woman?"

His sexy grin made her feel all fuzzy and warm, and she grinned back.

Without thought, her mouth met his as he pulled her to his body. The kiss was a mix of relief and fascination. No thought of bad men and what was good for her, she immersed herself in the taste and textures of the man in her arms. Pure liquid heat. She wanted him closer.

"For goodness' sakes, girl, let the boy come up for air."

Her mom's voice jerked her into reality. "And mercy, he's getting good ol' Alabama red dirt all over the floor. The living room looks like we had a mud-wrestling contest."

Good thing her mom interrupted when she had. What would they have been doing if she waited five minutes longer? For that matter, what was she doing kissing Luke? She needed to concentrate on protecting her mom and herself.

She stepped away but Luke held on. With a shake of her head, he released her with a groan.

"Sorry, mom," she said as she took another step back.

What else could she say? *I was thanking Luke for digging up my husband and retrieving the box you placed in his coffin by mistake?*

"What a cute teddy bear he got you." Her mom picked up the box and teddy. "What's the key for? His heart? It's too big for the little heart the bear is holding." Her teasing brought a warmth to Mary's face.

"Mom—"

"Mrs. Ford, your daughter was kind enough to accept a date with me this Friday, and I couldn't help but give her a small gift," Luke interrupted before she said too much.

Thank goodness, her mom had forgotten about the box she'd placed in Vince's coffin.

Luke smiled, reaching for the teddy and box.

Her mom released her hold. "Whose fist did you run into?"

"Just a friend helping out and getting carried away."

"Please leave Luke alone," Mary insisted.

"Well, Luke is getting blood and dirt all over my clean floors." Her mom eyed the lanky bad boy with one eyebrow raised. "Go into the bathroom, strip, and take a shower. When you're finished, I'll have you something to wrap around yourself until we get your clothes clean. Then I'll see to that eye and cut."

"No need. I'll head over to the house—"

"And have you scare your daddy with the cemetery dirt all over you?" The older woman shook her head. "You two thought I didn't remember the box. It's true, at first, I didn't recognize it."

"Did you know there was a teddy bear inside?" Had her mom looked inside before placing it in the coffin? Had her mom taken the papers out of the box?

"No. You had told me it was private. You were grieving. I didn't want to make it worse." She squeezed Mary's hand and then turned her attention to Luke, pointing down the hall. "You. Go. And before you step into that shower, throw your clothes in the hallway for me to wash."

Mary waited to see who would win the argument. Her money was on her mom.

Chapter Eighteen

Luke could tell from the stubborn look on the older woman's face there was no need to argue.

"Yes, ma'am."

He glanced at Mary as he walked away. The hungry look he received had his body answering with a need of its own. Damn, that woman had him feeling like a pervert with her mother only steps away.

Within seconds, he was under the spray of cold water, best for reining in his rampant libido, and his clothes in a pile outside the door. The cut on his cheek stung like a son of a bitch, reminding him of Trim's stone-hard fist. For a skinny little guy, he had a mean right hook.

It took only a twenty and a bottle of Jim Beam to talk Trim into letting him use the backhoe and take any heat if the law showed up. Trim had said he needed a day off and the jail was as good a place as any to spend it. At least he would get a couple of free meals and a day without his wife nagging at him.

Despite that Mary hadn't told him why she needed the box, it was obvious whatever was inside would protect her from Lazaro. He was glad to help her. He would dig up the whole county if she'd kiss him like she had moments earlier. For now, he'd just wait until she was ready to tell him the rest of her secrets.

As soon as he turned off the water, he heard Mrs. Ford say, "I left you a robe on the doorknob." He hoped it wasn't pink.

He cracked open the door. Not bad. He lifted the plain, baby-blue terry cloth robe. He sighed with relief. No lace or pink. Mrs. Ford was a well-rounded lady and thankfully her robe was large enough to work. The cloth showed some of his chest and ended at his knees but covered the essentials.

As he stepped into the kitchen, the two women at the table turned to stare. Mrs. Ford covered her mouth to stop a chuckle, while Mary took her time checking him out.

He concentrated on acting nonchalant as he made his way to a chair. Otherwise, the heat from her eyes would ensure a response that would embarrass everyone in the kitchen.

"If I say so myself, the robe brings the blue out in your eyes," said the older woman.

"Thank you, Mrs. Ford."

"Please, call me Alice. You're wearing my robe after all."

She coquettishly fluttered her eyelashes at him.

Luke's eyebrows rose nearly to his hairline.

"Mom. Quit trying to embarrass him. You know, some days I believe you live and breathe to torment me." The way Mary squished her lips together proved she was holding back a laugh.

Alice chuckled. "I'm merely declaring a fact." Her mom waved her off and turned to Luke. "You don't embarrass so easy, do you?"

"No, ma'am. I'm a southern boy through and through

and do indulge in a little flirting." Luke winked at Alice. "Like you said, I am wearing your robe." He adjusted the front. "Well, sort of."

Chapter Nineteen

Her mom laughed harder than Mary had seen her do in a couple of years.

Mary was glad he was a good sport. Yet, they needed to changed the subject, no matter how good he looked in the damp material.

She said, "Mom and I were talking while you were in the shower about the key on the teddy bear. We believe it fits something of Vinny's in Hicks's Storage Buildings."

Though enough time had passed for her to get rid of all the mementos, she struggled with letting go of her husband. She scooted back in the chair, straightening her shoulders. Maybe it was time now.

"Well, let's get my clothes and head there."

That was that. No questions of why she needed the key. Just simple acceptance of what she needed done. His willingness to help without question amazed her.

She watched him stand and head toward the laundry room door. The robe cupped his butt so lovingly, revealing a shape that any female would wish to grasp during a night of love making. The man had a nice ass.

"Your clothes aren't ready yet." Mary raised her voice. "Besides, the storage building is several miles away."

She liked how he looked in her kitchen. Hair tousled and barefoot, he glanced over his shoulder at her.

"That'll have to wait until tomorrow. I've got a doctor's appointment this afternoon and need Mary to take me. I can't drive anymore since the onset of my sickness. So you'll need to go tomorrow morning." Alice pointed to the chair next to her. "Come back here and have a seat. My girl can take care of your injuries."

Mary was glad her mom reminded them. She was beginning to wonder what Luke's face looked like without all the bruises and cuts.

Her mom turned to her. "I'll go and take a shower myself while you doctor Handsome."

Without further demands, Alice left the kitchen. Mary grabbed the medical supplies, opening the top of the red tin box. Taking a cotton swab, she coated it with an antibacterial cream and dabbed at the cut on his cheek. The swelling around his eye had nearly disappeared and only a little purple remained on one lid.

"You're fortunate someone hasn't hit you hard enough to damage your eye and make you lose your sight."

"That would be a shame."

Something about his tone brought her eyes to his. He was staring at her with a hunger that had nothing to do with food. She felt her cheeks grow hot. Her gaze dropped to his hands resting on the table. Long fingers with scabs across the knuckles on one hand, various scars covering both. Hands belonging to a man who kept busy.

"You didn't hit Trim." She couldn't resist lifting his hand and skimming her fingers across the healing wounds at least a day old.

"Nah. He only did what I needed. He just got carried away."

His fingers remained relaxed beneath her touch. Mary wasn't sure how long they stayed silent, staring at each others' hands, but they jumped when her mom walked into the room.

"You two are as nervous as cats in a roomful of rockers." Mary felt her mom's stare as she released his hands and stood.

"Guess we need to get going if we don't want to be late to the appointment," Mary said.

Seeing Luke sitting at her kitchen table, relaxed with a barely there grin, she came to a conclusion. She was wrong. Yes, he was a bad boy, but so unlike Vinny.

Violence had been a big part of Vinny's life, but also a part of who he'd been. He'd been energized after a fight or a risky job. Thankfully, violence hadn't spilled over into their married life though some of their arguments had been on the edge.

Then there was Luke. He responded with violence only when cornered and nowhere to go. The times she'd seen him after a fight, he'd been pensive, even a little disturbed by the results. He was different and she was glad.

"I'll finish up painting the family room and start on the kitchen," he said.

He stood and grabbed the back of the chair. His face paled.

"Look at you. You're about to pass out. Don't worry about painting." She grabbed his arm and helped him back into his seat. Mary began to tick off her fingers. "Let's see, this week you've been bit by Sally, slammed by Evil, and left-hooked by Trim. Plus Chet and his cousins had a go at you. I'll say you deserve some time off."

"Who told you about Chet's cousins?"

"Susan mentioned Chet sicced those behemoth monsters on you." Unable to resist, she brushed the hair out of his eyes. The strands were cool, still a little damp from his shower. "Stay here and rest. We'll be back in a few hours. Mom has promised to cook her world-famous chicken and dumplings tonight."

"I'll be here."

She liked the sound of that, knowing he'd be waiting for her.

Chapter Twenty

Luke straightened after opening the first can of Wales Green. He shook his head. Who made up these strange names for light green? He double-checked the walls, making sure the blue tape covered the necessary areas. In the hour after pulling his clothes back on, he'd taped off the kitchen and prepared it for painting. No way could he sit around and wait. He needed something to do. So he decided to paint. That was what they had hired him to do. If he became dizzy, he would sit down until it passed.

"Hey, Lu, you there?"

Luke sighed. That was the last thing he needed.

"In here, Evil." Out of the corner of his eye, he noticed the teddy bear sitting in the middle of the table. No time to stash it somewhere. He took comfort in knowing Evil would have no idea of its importance.

"Man, good to see some woman can get you to work." Evil walked over to the table and pulled out a chair. His long legs encased in dirty Levi's stretched out over the floor as he leaned back folding his hands behind his head. "You going to the Sandbox tonight? Smooth wants to win his fifty back."

As his brother mentioned his name, Smooth walked into the kitchen. There was something spooky about Evil's brother. Rather ironic as Smooth had the least-threatening name. It was just, the man was too quiet. He'd always heard the quiet ones needed to be watched, something about doing too much thinking and letting anger build up.

The fair-haired man nodded his head in greeting.

Luke nodded back and turned his attention to Evil. "Nah. I think I'll hang around here. Do some work."

His involvement with Mary was nobody's business but his and Mary's. Evil had issues with women, what with his mom running off and something about a girl doing him dirty years ago. It was best to keep his friend's opinion out of it.

"So it's like that, huh?"

"What do you mean?" Luke lifted the can of paint and poured some in the roller pan, hoping his work would speed up their departure. Neither was known for being hard-working since coming back to their hometown.

Evil pointed to the bear. "Buying her girly gifts. What's the key to?" Luke froze. "To your heart?" Evil added and then began to laugh.

Luke picked up the roller. "If you fellows don't want to help, I suggest you head on over to the Sandbox without me."

"Sorry, man, didn't mean to make fun of your taste in presents." His dark-headed friend shifted in his chair. "We also wanted to tell you that Smooth and I got your back. We're keeping an eye out for any strangers coming around and staying. Lazaro's still in Vegas. I have a couple buddies who live there and owe me a couple favors. If he makes a move to come here, I'll know before he gets in his stretch limo."

Feeling bad for his uncharitable thoughts from a moment earlier, he reminded himself that no matter the two men were a pain in the butt, they always looked out for him. He knew if it hadn't been for the Rogan brothers, Chet and his cousins would've kicked Luke's ass out of town or put him six feet under long ago.

"I appreciate that. More than you can know," said Luke.

Evil stood and turned toward the door. "Just be careful. Let me know anything that I can do that'll keep you safe. Okay?"

Luke almost called them back to get their opinion on the teddy bear. But a bad feeling, like Evil and Smooth were holding something back from him, kept his mouth shut.

Chapter Twenty-One

Mary was in hell.

While the doctor performed tests on her mother, she'd remained in the waiting room, worrying what else the doctor would find. About forty-five minutes into the appointment, who walked in but Betsy Twilldale and Sue Marie Coleman. She shouldn't be surprised considering Dr. Johnson was the only geriatrician in Sand City.

If only she could think of an excuse to leave.

"Well, hello, Mrs. Hightower. I see you're waiting for the doctor too." Betsy smoothed the seat of her skirt as she sat across from Mary, knees and ankles together with feet to one side. All proper and lady's academy trained.

"Actually, I'm—"

"Sue Marie just refuses to come alone." Betsy folded her hands in her lap.

"I just detest doctors and their nosey questions." Sue Marie leaned forward as if imparting a secret.

Mary lost her voice. One of the tattling twosomes

talking about doctors being nosey? This was the pot calling the kettle black for sure.

"Sorry to hear about your husband." The way Betsy eyed her, Mary knew she wanted more to gossip about.

"I'm not sure I know what you mean?" Always best to play dumb. Safer that way.

Sue Marie touched her arm. "You know, how Luke dug up your husband's grave."

"Oh. The sheriff told me Mr. Posey did that." Mary had to protect Luke. She rolled the magazine in her lap. What would the two gossips think if she hit them on their noses like two irresponsible puppies?

"We know that's what Bubba's telling everyone. He's always taking up for Luke. One of these days we'll figure out what that boy has on the sheriff." Betsy pulled at the hem of her skirt, covering her knees.

Sue Marie looked around. "It's a crazy stunt for sure. He's a lot like his ma. She spent three months in the loony bin at Tuscaloosa for depression. Less than a month after she got out she was dead."

Betsy placed her hand next to her mouth, keeping others on one side of the room from seeing her lips move. "Luke did it."

That burned Mary's drawers. How could they know that for sure? "I thought the reason Luke spent time in prison was for burglary."

"That's the only crime he was caught at. He found it rather hard to explain how the two computers got in the back of his truck. They came from Fred's Electronics. Bubba and Fred found Luke passed out on the side of the road with the computers in the back." Betsy sighed. "He got off light and only because Bubba stood up for him."

The older woman shook her head.

So that was what happened. Could the old biddies not see that anyone could arrange for the computers to be found? Mary had seen plenty people inebriated, and when they passed out, anything could be done to them. Usually, they had their pockets picked, not set up for a felony. The price of the computers was probably over the five-hundred-dollar limit for petty theft.

She would regret this, especially as the ladies' information was often faulty, but she wanted to know the town's version.

"Why do you say Luke killed his mom?"

Betsy turned to Sue Marie. "You tell her."

"Okay. Ruth and I just happened to be coming to visit when I heard the scream—Ruth's almost deaf as a post. What do I see when I run in? Why, Luke Blackwood sitting on the floor holding his mama's head in his lap, rocking back and forth. Blood was all over him and the floor. He kept saying, 'I'm sorry, Mama. I'm so sorry.' It was a sad scene for sure."

Sue Marie pulled a tissue from her purse and blew her nose.

"Just because he was holding her, wouldn't mean he killed her. Where was Mr. Blackwood?"

Betsy and Sue Marie looked at each other and appeared to come to a decision.

Sue Marie dabbed at the corner of one eye.

"He'd been out in the field. He came running in behind me and Ruth. By the time the sheriff, that was Joe Freeman then, came, Reverend Blackwood had cleaned up Luke, his wife, and the floor. Ruth and I argued about that, but there was no stopping the Reverend."

"What was the decision on her death?" Mary really

hated herself for listening to them. She felt disloyal to a man that had done nothing but help her.

"They said she had a massive stroke, killed her as she stood."

"What about the blood?"

"She'd hit her head on the corner of the coffee table as she went down."

"Well, that explained everything. I don't understand why you believe Luke killed her."

Thankfully, the waiting room had almost emptied out and only a handful had heard. The two women enjoyed passing on such a sad story and Mary wished she hadn't asked.

"I guess because he told everyone he did," Betsy answered with a huff.

"He was a twelve-year-old kid, he probably blamed himself for it."

"Hey, Mary. Ladies." Susan greeted them before anymore could be said. She sat next to Mary and smiled. "Sue Marie, your name has been called twice since I walked into the waiting room."

Sue Marie hurried to the receptionist's desk, waving Betsy to follow.

"Thank goodness. Why couldn't the receptionist have called them sooner?" Mary slumped in her chair. Her body ached from the tension of hearing enough gossip to last a lifetime.

"Those old bags can be useful at times, huh?" Susan leaned toward Mary. "I thought you and Luke were just friends? I didn't know friends bought friends teddy bears."

"Sheriffs can be useful too, right?" She lifted an eyebrow at her friend.

It was rough when she couldn't trust her own sheriff to keep his mouth shut. Who had Susan talked to? They had become friends on the first day after arriving in town. Then again, she had known Luke for half that time and she trusted him more.

"You've got to admit, that's some good lowdown. Bubba said the bear had a key around his neck. What else did that crazy bad boy buy you?"

Mary didn't like how Susan questioned her about the private part of her life. Maybe she was overreacting. The years with Vinny and his cautionary lifestyle had influenced her more than she thought.

"Only the key to his heart."

Old habits were hard to break. There she went lying again.

Before guilt could start eating at her, her mother walked into the waiting room. Normally Mary would talk with the doctor herself, but today were just tests. They would come back in two weeks and the doctor would call then.

"Mom, you remember Susan from the diner."

"Oh, yes, Bubba's hot tomato."

"Mom!"

Chapter Twenty-Two

"Thank you, Mrs. Ford, for a wonderful dinner. I believe that's the best chicken and dumplings I've ever tasted."

Luke pushed away from the table and groaned. At the rate these two ladies were stuffing him, he would be ready to sit in as Santa for Christmas.

"Why, thank you, Handsome." Alice looked so happy and lucid. "Since you two probably would like to be alone, I'll leave you to clean the kitchen while I watch TV."

"Sorry. Mom can be..." Mary shrugged her shoulders and picked up his plate, stacking it on the others.

She had a fragile look to her, her shoulders rounded, not the usual proud straight back. Between worrying about her husband's ex-boss and her mom, the pressures must be pulling her down.

He stood and walked behind her to grasp her shoulders. All the tension beneath his fingers relaxed. When she leaned back, he slid one hand across her chest above her soft breasts and the other hand beneath, pressing her to his length. The light smell of honeysuckle teased his nose. He liked that about her. When he held her in his arms, he felt like he was where he belonged. Even though it was early fall, he almost expected a light summer breeze. Drawn to the exposed length of her long, smooth neck, he leaned down and kissed the pulsing skin, and then his tongue skated behind her ear.

Her groan brought a grin to his face. He nuzzled the sensitive area behind her ear, and she dropped her head onto his shoulder. She clasped his hands. Before he realized what she planned, she placed them over her breasts. Encouraged by her action and the taut nubs beneath his palms, he pinched and alternatively rubbed the hard tips as he massaged what he wanted to taste.

Her hip nestled against his groin and she began to undulate in a dance of need. He groaned and answered her rhythm with one of his own. He was so hard, he knew with one touch of her heat he would dissolve in a puddle of desire. Mercy, the woman was about to kill him.

The thought of Mary, face first, on the table as he took her from behind almost made him lose it.

How in the world he did it, he wasn't sure, but the next thing he knew he was standing on the other side of the table, staring at her. She'd turned around, chest heaving—damn, she looked good—and licking her lips. Her flushed faced told him she couldn't believe he stopped either. Then she sighed, probably realizing how close she'd come to making love to an ex-convict.

"God, Mary. Your ma's in the other room. No matter how much she likes me, I don't think she would be happy if I fucked her daughter in the kitchen."

His chest felt so tight, and if he didn't know better, he would believe he was having a heart attack. But he knew that was impossible as his heart was throbbing in his pants.

"She's probably sound asleep. All it takes is for her to sit in front of the tube and she's out like a light." She rubbed her hands along the sides of her dress pants.

"You know, I might need to stay, to keep an eye on things." He was so full of it.

She swallowed. Was she still turned on or afraid of what he would do next?

"I appreciate the offer but I'll set the alarm. We'll be safe."

Scum. He was pond scum. What was he thinking? Pushing himself on a lady like her? Yeah, she'd been a show-girl, but he knew a lady when he saw one, held one. She was a lady outside and deep inside.

Of course, the way she placed his hands on her breasts wasn't exactly genteel, but she'd been without her husband for almost two years and even a lady needed relief. He knew how hard it had been on him during almost the same length of time in prison. Anyone would help her. This see-sawing of emotions drove him crazy.

"I'll help you clean up and then get out." He turned to pick up the bowls.

"No need. I'll take care of it."

He stopped.

"Dammit, Mary, I'm sorry. I know I was out of line."

"There's nothing to be sorry about."

He turned to her. She'd crossed her arms as if to protect herself.

"I can't say it won't happen again. I want you." There he said it. He had to let her know the lay of the land. "I want to taste every inch of your skin."

"It's probably best that you leave."

"What about tomorrow? Can't you trust me?" He clinched his jaw.

She stared at him. Was she wrestling with her feelings?

"Have I blown it?" He waited for her answer.

"No. You haven't. I'm just a little..." She sighed. "I don't know. I just know I need a little time to think. You're one more straw than I'd bargained for lately and I..." Tears welled up in her eyes. "I want to sleep on it."

"Okay." He turned to leave and stopped. Without looking back, he said, "I'll keep my window open. If your alarm goes off, I'll be here in two minutes tops."

Nothing. Silence. It didn't matter. If she wanted his help or not, she got it.

"Sorry." Then he left.

<<<>>>

"Hey, Lu! Wake up!"

Luke covered his head with a pillow.

"I know you're awake now. Come to the window and talk with me."

"Dammit! Evil! What's your problem? Can't you let an honest man get a good night's sleep?"

Luke twisted his sheet around his waist and walked over to the window.

"Man, I'm not used to you going to sleep at nine f-ing o'clock in the evening." Evil folded his arms on the windowsill and grinned.

"I got a job. Why don't you get one?" Luke glanced at his clock and leaned against the wall. "And it's five after midnight.

"I do what needs to be done." He looked around Luke's

room. "How about getting some clothes on and coming to the Sandbox? Since you've got job security and all, you can pay."

"Go away, Evil." Luke shook his head and crawled into bed, giving his back to his friend. "Get a life!"

"You're just not any fun anymore." Evil chuckled. "I got to tell you something."

"I don't want to know."

"Come on, it's good stuff."

Luke cracked an eye at Evil. "What?"

Evil hesitated and then said, "You won't believe this, but I just saw the funniest thing. Bubba and Susan in the county SUV necking near the river. I wonder if that's against the law?"

Luke threw his pillow, hitting the wall next to the window. "Go away. Everyone knows about them." A few minutes passed and Luke relaxed. Evil could be rather insistent at times.

Was it merely minutes or hours later Luke jerked wide awake? A buzzing in the background hauled him out of his bed. Mary's house alarm. He grabbed his jeans and pulled them on as he stepped into his unlaced gym shoes. Seconds later he was out the door with one arm in an old flannel shirt.

He crossed the pasture at a dead run while zipping his pants. The cool fall air brought chill bumps across his chest as his open shirt flapped behind him. With one hand on the top rail, he jumped over the fence next to Mary's backyard. The laces on his shoes slapped his jeans legs with each step.

All the lights were on in her house. He tried the back door. Locked. He banged on the screen's wood frame as he shouted, "Let me in, Mary! It's Luke."

The door crashed open as Mary stepped back, fear and anger glittering in her eyes.

"It's mom! She said she heard someone. The alarm didn't go off until he opened the front door and ran out."

Luke took off and flew through the still-open front door. He saw no cars or any evidence of someone nearby. In the distance he heard tires squeal. He returned to the house to find Mary kneeling next to her mom on the couch.

"I probably shouldn't have moved her, but I wasn't about to leave her on the floor." Mary swiped at the tears streaming down her face.

"I'm okay." Alice's words slurred as she squeezed her daughter's fingers.

"What happened?" Deep inside he knew he should've stayed with her.

Panting from his run, he stood over the women, hands on his hips. He would kill the bastard.

Chapter Twenty-Three

Not until tonight had Mary realized how much she missed having a man in the house.

She looked at Luke, shirt open, bare chest lifting and falling from his sprint across the pasture to her house. His forehead wrinkled from concern. Mary knew not just any man would do.

She turned and checked her mom's pallid face. With trembling fingers, Mary brushed her mom's hair from her eyes.

"I heard her scream and then a series of thumps. When I came down the stairs, she was lying at the bottom. I'll never get the picture out of my head."

"I'm okay, sweetie." Her mom clumsily wiped her mouth, the left corner drooping. "He only scared me and before I knew it, I tumbled down a couple steps. I didn't hear any of my old bones crunching."

"Oh, sweet Lord, Mom." She refused to think what could've happened. The signs of a stroke were bad enough.

"Did he say anything?" Luke asked.

"No. I just saw someone dressed in dark clothes coming

out of the kitchen." Every other word was slurred but spoken clearly enough for Mary to understand. "You better check to see if they stole our good silverware."

Mary shook her head. They could steal anything they wanted as long as her mother was okay. Then it hit her: the teddy bear.

Luke called 911 while she slipped a sofa pillow beneath her mom's head. Then Mary hurried into the kitchen. The teddy bear was still there on the baker's rack where she'd placed it the day before.

So stupid to think they would leave her alone until the arranged meeting. She remembered their method. She picked up the soft bear and smoothed the fur down its plump back.

"Oh, no." She stared at the bear in horror.

In seconds, Luke clasped her shoulder, pulling her into his warm embrace. "What's wrong?"

"The key's gone."

<<<>>>

"Are you sure we did the right thing?" Mary closed her eyes tight, the oncoming headlights hurting her tired eyes.

"Your mom insisted you go home and get some rest. I agree with her."

She turned her head on the seat to argue with him, but was sidetracked by how good he looked driving her car. Then passing street lights flickered across his face, giving her small glimpses of the circles around his eyes and fine lines around his mouth. He was tired too.

The hours they'd spent in Brookwood Hospital, checking in her mom and waiting for the doctors to answer her questions, had taken their toll. Thankfully they expected her mom to recover fully. A small stroke, they'd said. Like that would make her worry less. The numbness had dissipated within a couple of hours, and the cardiologist planned to hold her for observation and tests for a few more days, the miracle of science and insurance plans.

During the long day they spent at the hospital, Luke never questioned her again about the missing key or why it was so important. Or did he already know? Had his friend Evil provided more information Luke hadn't divulged? No. Something deep inside told her he had nothing to do with it. She needed to keep trusting him. There was no one else. Her mom was in no position to help.

Another glance at Luke's profile, his five o'clock shadow, and his all-business look, brought an odd question to mind.

"How old are you?"

Masculine, thick brows dipped into a vee as he shot a look at her.

"Why? Am I looking old?"

She chuckled. "No. That's up to what you consider old?"

Vinny had been twelve years older. In fact, his age had been part of the reason her mom disliked him in the beginning. He'd robbed the cradle in her mom's eyes. Mary had been nineteen when they met and twenty-two when they'd married.

"I'll be twenty-five November fifteenth." He cut his eyes toward her. "And you?"

"Twenty-seven." She'd guessed wrong. She'd thought him to be older. Something to do with the slight smile wrinkles at the corner of his eyes. She grinned.

"I'm dating an older woman." He smiled back. "What's your birthdate?"

"July sixteenth."

"For two more months you'll be three years older." He winked and then asked, "How about a quiet dinner at Bill's?"

The hour spent traveling behind the ambulance to the hospital had taken forever. Time dragged while they waited for the doctor, and then tests, and finally the diagnosis. And now the trip back to Sand City flew by. Amazing how Luke helped keep her mind off her worries about her mom.

The sun had been up for hours and the quick energy they'd gained from their snacks had waned away. She wanted food more than sleep.

Her stomach growled.

"I guess that's your answer."

"Food it is."

"Before we arrive, we should talk about the missing key, right?" Mary closed her eyes and leaned her head back.

"Yeah."

She cut her eyes toward Luke.

"You don't sound certain."

"I am. You said your husband's things are in the storage building. If we looked everything over, we should find something that requires a key."

"That makes sense. We can always force it open."

"We'll keep our fingers crossed that someone hasn't beaten us to it."

"There are hundreds of storage rental companies all in and around Birmingham. It would take them forever." She inhaled, a little relieved with that thought.

"But they know your alias."

"True." She covered her eyes with a hand. "Why do I

feel like we're digging at this with a teaspoon and everyone else is using a shovel?"

"We need a good night's rest to clear our mind. Tomorrow, maybe something with come to you while looking through his things."

She nodded, too tired to rehash everything that had happened the last few days in the hope of remembering clues she missed.

He tenderly clasped her hand. His rough palm indicated he wasn't afraid of hard work of any kind. Squeezing his fingers in appreciation, it was comforting to know Luke was there with her.

A few minutes later they turned into the nearly empty parking lot. It was too late for lunch but early still for the evening meal. In no time, they were seated and looking over the menu.

"Hello there, Mary. Luke." Susan stood next to the table, pen and pad in hand. "Sorry to hear about your mom. How's she doing?"

Mary began to tear up. She cleared her throat and smiled at her friend. "She's resting and should make a full recovery. Thanks for asking."

That was all she could say without making a fool of herself. She was never good at emotional scenes in front of people.

They ordered the same meal, hamburgers all the way, and sat in silence. She wished she could say they were comfortable with the quiet at their booth. She wanted to say a witty comment about the weather or tease about his pants being unsnapped until they arrived in the emergency room. Only she'd never been one of those silly frilly girls, batting their eyes and impressing guys with sarcastic humor.

Every inch of her body was keyed up and aware of

him. She reveled in his masculine scent, soap and an unidentifiable pleasant fragrance uniquely his own. His energy radiated across the table, pulling her toward his warmth. She wanted to touch those long fingers and feel their strength against her skin. Instead, she forced her eyes to stare unseeing out of the diner into the dark streets. Wild, undisciplined men were bad for her. Though Luke had proven he wasn't all bad. Nor was Vincent. Not really. There was so much more she wanted to know about him.

In the reflection of the window, she watched Susan slide chilled glasses of tea onto their table.

When Susan hesitated, instead of tending to the other people, Mary looked up, taking a sip of her tea. Whatever the woman had to say, she obviously wasn't sure how to come out with it.

"Everything okay?" Mary asked.

"What are you two now? A couple?"

Mary set the glass down and tucked her hands into her lap. She involuntarily released a sigh. Susan really tried to be a friend, but now wasn't one of those times.

Her frosty attitude was unexpected but not surprising.

"Luke was kind enough to stay with me while we waited for the doctor to check on Mom." Frowning, she looked over at Luke, his blank expression saying more than he realized. He expected her to deny their friendship. "And I appreciate his company and support."

"Just remember when it's all said and done, you can't say I didn't warn you."

"Susan." Saddened by her friend's attitude, Mary reached for her arm, but the woman ignored her and walked over to the take-out counter. Bubba stood waiting for her as he leaned one hip on a stool and nodded at Mary.

Luke grabbed Mary's hand, drawing her attention back to him.

"I'm sorry. As long as you hang around me, people will expect the worst."

"Hey, you never worked Vegas," she said in a low tone.

"That rough?" As he held her fingers, he traced the blue veins on the back of her hand.

Breathing became harder to manage as she'd always been a touchy-feely person. To have someone rub her back, arms, hands, feet or any part of her body soothed nerves better than any little pink pill. Though soothing was the last thing she felt when Luke caressed her. She wanted to strip him and lick every inch of his firm, lanky body.

Amazing how a touch of his hand had her completely forgetting the people watching her in the diner. She realized she hadn't answered his question. Her mind had wandered to more sensual things.

"No worse than any other area of entertainment." Her voice came out short of breath, her gaze roaming his beautiful face and body. "People will do anything to get ahead. After Vincent and I were married for a few months, we decided it would be best for me to stay home."

"He was tired of beating up assholes."

"Yeah. How did you guess?"

"I would have a hard time letting other men look at my wife parading on a stage in tight clothes smaller than most underwear."

"That rarely bothered him." She grinned. "Vinny grew up on the Las Vegas strip. He understood it was all an act. It was after the show when all the tourists thought we were free game. That drove him crazy."

Every so often there would be one idiot waiting for her outside the casino. Vincent could have an arm around her shoulders and that still didn't stop them from making obscene offers.

The possessive look in Luke's eyes sent a warm feeling across her torso. No matter how much she fought her feelings for the bad boy across the table, she knew there was more to him than a troublemaker. She'd seen the guilt and worry about doing the right thing cross Luke's face. Vinny never felt guilt over his actions, his job. He'd only wanted out because of his fear of losing her, of getting her hurt.

Before she could say anything else, Susan brought their hamburgers and fries. Without a word, she slapped the plates in front of them and rolled her eyes at Mary.

Surprised by her friend's action, she laughed.

"What happened?" He eyed the hamburger with suspicion.

"Nothing. I have a feeling Susan's not mad at me any more." She glanced over to the take-out counter as Bubba said something to Susan, causing the blonde to giggle. "And we might have Bubba to thank for her improved mood."

Chapter Twenty-Four

Luke watched Bubba whisper into Susan's ear.

"That reminds me. Evil said that Bubba and Susan were making out near the river last night," he said without taking his eyes off the sheriff.

"Yeah, they're hot for each other. Everyone knows that."

Mary took a large bite of her hamburger. Seeing a gentle woman take a mouthful like that turned him on. He imagined she would enjoy taking a large bite out of life, living large in ways he'd been denying himself for thirteen years.

He took a huge bite of his burger and grinned at Mary.

When she smile back and started to laugh, she covered her mouth to keep the food where it belonged.

"But why make out at the river? They both have their own places. A hell of lot more private and comfortable than a field." The lettuce crunched as he bit into his sandwich again. He savored the flavors of crisp lettuce, tart tomato, and juicy meat slathered with mayo. Bill knew how to put together a hamburger.

She stopped chewing and looked at him with chocolate

eyes wide open. "You think they had something to do with the break-in?"

"Maybe." He took another bite of his sandwich as he concentrated on the possibilities. Over half of the hamburger was gone before he added, "There's also Evil and Smooth."

"Did you hear something?"

"Evil came by the house last night. Usually wherever he goes, his brother isn't far behind. But Smooth didn't show up."

"What time?"

"Midnight. He's the one who told me about Bubba and Susan parking." His shoulders tensed. The only time he felt like this was when he knew something bad was about to happen.

"Hey, Luke Blackwood. Did you try to kill your girl-friend's ma like you did yours?" Chet Macon stood in the middle of the diner, fists clenched at his side.

Luke shot out of the booth and grabbed the man by the shirt. Nose to nose, he glared into the man's eyes.

"Apologize," he said between clenched teeth in an effort to keep his voice low, not wanting to disturb the restaurant's patrons more than they'd already been by Chet's insolent question.

"To you or her? It's the truth, isn't it?" Pure contempt poured from the man's mouth.

A bolt of light and pain flashed across Luke's eyes. The asshole's right hook snapped his head to the side. Drums pounded in his ears as the world came into focus.

As if in slow motion, Luke slammed a fist into the scum's face. Blood spurted from Chet's nose.

Screams echoed and chaos consumed what happened next. Numerous hands grabbed Luke by the arms and neck, pulling him away from doing more damage. Other men were doing the same to Chet.

"Stop it!" Bubba had Luke's right arm in his grasp.

"I'm calm, I'm calm," Chet said with palms held out at his waist. The men stupidly released him. Chet punched Luke in the stomach.

Pain drilled a hole to his spine.

"Dammit, Bubba. Let me go!" Luke wheezed between each sentence in a vain attempt to catch his breath.

"No," the sheriff said to Luke. "Chet, you hit him again, I'm arresting you. We're holding Luke and that's not fighting fair."

When would Bubba ever learn? Chet didn't know the meaning.

The next jab had Luke choking on his supper. Shouting and crashing of chairs sounded far away at the same time as a reverberating boom.

That sounded like gunfire. Someone had shot off a gun in the restaurant? Then he heard the strangest thing.

"Chet, if you hit him one more time, you will be singing a note so high, the dogs will think you're calling them."

Mary stood, one hand clasping the other holding a small pistol aimed at Chet. She looked awfully comfortable holding the weapon. Yeah, she knew how to handle a gun. Her husband had taught her well. Considering how he'd been getting his butt beat, he didn't really care at the moment.

"Arrest the bitch!" Chet's florid face turned a beet red as he waited for the sheriff to act.

When Bubba finally released him, Luke turned to the sheriff. "Don't touch her." Nose-to-nose, he added, "Remember, you owe me."

Without looking at her, Bubba asked, "Mrs. Hightower,

did you believe someone was threatening to do you or someone you know bodily harm?"

"Yes."

"Unless Susan wants to press charges against Mrs. Hightower for damaging her ceiling, I would say I have no reason to arrest her." The sheriff glanced at Susan and stepped away.

"Susan, I'll pay for the damage." Mary's eyes widened, pleading for her to understand.

"Bill is needing a new roof," Susan remarked with a teasing light in her eyes.

"Done," Mary said as if she was talking about replacing a window.

How much money did that woman have?

Luke turned to Chet. "You better leave now while the getting's good. Next time I see you, there won't be anything left for your wife to pick up," he said in a soft voice, more threatening with the calmness he delivered it.

Chet looked around, seeing only hostile faces. No help from anyone at the diner. The late afternoon blinds on the door crashed against the glass as he slammed it behind him.

"Are you okay?"

Luke turned to Mary. He noticed the gun was out of sight, back in her purse. The sheepish look on her face almost had him laughing. He didn't care if a woman saved his ass.

He grabbed her elbow. "Let's get out of here before Bubba changes his mind." He threw money on the table and stepped outside, still holding her arm.

"What does he owe you for?"

He shook his head and opened the diner's door and then later the passenger's door for Mary.

"I think you need to answer some questions of your

own." She stood staring at him. He stared back. "Get in. We'll talk at your house."

"Okay. I understand you're upset. You're right, we have a lot to talk about." She slipped into the seat and he gently closed the door. No need to take his anger out on such a nice car.

"We just need to talk." Why didn't she understand what could've happened back there?

The few miles to the house brought little relief to his worry and anger. He blamed himself for trying to make her into what he wanted. The woman was no angel and had as much baggage as he did. Somehow he needed to listen. But every time he saw in his mind's eye her holding that pistol, he thought of what could've happened. Cold chills ran down his back. The hell with her already knowing how to shoot a gun, what was he thinking when he encouraged her to carry one? Had he wanted her to get killed? What was she thinking? The vicious cycle would drive him crazy.

He waited until she opened the door and locked it behind them, turning the security alarm back on. Once she placed her purse with the gun inside on the coffee table, he grabbed her by the arms and pressed her back to the wall.

"You are something, did you know that? I don't know many women who would pull a gun in public to save their man," he said, his voice steady and strong. One step had his lanky body touching hers. His heart thumping his chest so hard, he was certain a heart attack was imminent.

"I do what's necessary." She trailed the edge of her hand down his cheek.

"I want you so much." He skimmed her bottom lip with his thumb. So soft. If anything had happened to her... He shied away from finishing the thought.

Her sharp teeth nipped at the pad of his thumb. Being

near her, touching her, made him forget his reasons for being angry.

"The feeling is mutual. I hate to admit, whenever you hit Chet, I become so turned on, I have to squeeze my knees together." She leaned into his body, her lips only a breath away.

Damn. Hearing her say how his wild side affected her made him hard in appreciation. The woman in his arms was warm, the scent of honeysuckle teasing his senses.

He took her mouth and explored what he wanted to taste again, craved for a lifetime since they last kissed. She met his tongue with an obvious need of her own. When he eased away, her fingers grabbed handfuls of hair and pulled his mouth back to hers. He liked that she'd lost control and wanted to see how far he could push her.

Sinking into her soul-searching kiss, he slipped a hand beneath her blouse and cupped a breast. A slight shift of his hip brought a respite to his tight jeans. He was sure he'd burst from the need to be inside her. Dropping kisses down her chin and along her neck, unable to resist, he jerked her bra down, a taut nipple bursting free. His fingers pinched the hard nubs, then he licked, sucked one morsel, wanting her gasps to turn to cries of intense pleasure.

She had plans of her own. He'd been so immersed in touching her, she'd unbuttoned his shirt, unsnapped his jeans, and was working on the zipper without him being aware. Somehow he needed to slow down their madness. He didn't have a condom and, if he went any further, there would be no stopping.

One soft hand dipped behind his waistband and squeezed his erection. He groaned. She dragged her breasts down his chest.

"Mary. Honey. Stop." Her mouth latched onto a masculine nipple, her tongue swirling the hard knot in a way he would promise her anything to not stop. "You're killing me. Want between your legs. Don't have protection. Do you?"

He seriously thought about getting on his knees and praying she would say yes. Then again, a wide variety of possibilities in heaven could be found on his knees.

"Nooooo," she said in despair.

That did it. On his knees was as close to heaven as he would get that evening. He might not find release, but he wanted this woman trembling in his arms with the satisfaction he could provide. The mere thought of tasting her and knowing he could make her come almost pushed him over the edge. He jerked her pants and panties off. The tight curls, trimmed and glistening with need, beckoned to his need to taste every flavor she offered. His mouth covered the beginning swell of her pussy. He tongued and nibbled the protuberance and savored her heat.

This was as close to heaven as he would ever get.

Chapter Twenty Five

As heat engulfed her, Mary took another deep breath to keep from fainting. The delicious treatment provided by the man between her thighs had her heart pulsating throughout her body. His head bobbed with each thrust of his tongue. His fingers dug into her buttocks. Any discomfort barely registered as he sucked the stiff nub, pulling her closer to orgasm, and when she was about to let go, he licked and nipped at the over-sensitized bundle of nerves.

She locked her knees to keep from falling. The man possessed skills she'd never imagined.

When her legs began to tremble, he lifted her onto his shoulders, her back leaning against the wall, and finished what he started. She came, body arching and mouth silently open.

"Let go of my hair, Honey."

She liked the way he said Honey, deep and smooth as honey itself. As no one else ever had. But she still preferred Mary.

She unclenched her aching fingers, though she wanted his mouth between her legs again. Badly. Never had she experienced such an orgasm. Vince had been good, but... hmm...Luke's mouth was great. Scratch that. It was stupendous, wonderful, awesome, magnificent... She was certain the smile on her face gave away what she felt better than any adjective she could come up with.

Using the strength he'd shown her earlier, he eased her to the floor until she stood on her own two feet.

"Sorry," she muttered belatedly.

Talk about letting herself go. Embarrassment flooded warmth across her face, not from what they had done but from her loss of control.

When she peeked up at him through her eyelashes, she noted his stillness. He stood with his arms to the side, shirt opened and the swollen tip of his penis peeking out of his unzipped pants. Her eyelids slid half closed in pure delight at the vision.

He cleared his throat.

"I'm not. Sorry, that is," he said.

She dragged her gaze from the delectable sight of his cock.

"I have condoms in my bedroom," she said, her voice croaking on the last word.

"I thought you said you didn't have protection." His bad-boy-type grin, dimpled and full of meaning, caused her mouth to almost drool with need.

She swallowed.

"At the time, my bedroom was too far away." Why was he wasting time talking? The bedroom wasn't getting any closer.

"Lead the way," he offered.

As she walked up the stairs, she remembered that she wore only an unsnapped bra and wrinkled blouse. She peeked behind her, and as she suspected, he watched her naked bottom sashay at eye level. Swaying her hips, she put on her best performance.

"If you don't hurry, we'll say the hell with the condoms and take our chances. And no matter how good fucking on the stairs looks in the movies, it's not."

She ran up the stairs, laughing.

He caught her in the doorway of her bedroom and tossed her on top of the mattress. Before she landed from the bounce, he caught her, and then tossed her bra and blouse to the side. She wiggled from beneath him enough to grab a condom from the nightstand, tearing it open with a flare that brought his dimpled bad-boy grin back.

As he thrust into her heat, she gasped. *Perfect.* He powered into her over and over again. No need to urge him on. He lifted his chest off hers but she pulled him back, scraping his ribs with her nails in her attempt to remain close.

"I fit tight and perfect," he whispered in her ear.

"I was thinking the same thing." The words came out in a near whisper.

She struggled to make it last longer and gave up when he bent down and sucked hard on her nipple. Her scream of pleasure echoed off the walls as each surge hit her. The world dimmed.

Hours later, after another round of the best sex she'd ever had, she sucked in the cool evening air, trying to feed her starving lungs. The man did take her breath away.

For the first time in eighteen months, the shadows dancing on the ceiling didn't bring fear creeping into her belly.

She snuggled against the firm, masculine chest. Her hand blindly traced his rib cage to hipbone, coming to rest in the tight curls at his groin. Without looking, she knew he was ready again.

And she was too.

Chapter Twenty-Six

"That's it!"

Luke warily scanned the storage building Mary pointed to behind an empty car lot. Like most facilities of the same ilk, the deserted area looked a little worse for wear. Weeds grew near the edge of the metal buildings and along the chain-link fence. The access in front of each locked garage-style door needed a new load of gravel as it had more the look of hard-packed dirt.

As soon as she unlocked the heavy-duty padlock, he pushed up the rattling door, grimacing as the rusty rollers squealed in protest.

Mary covered her mouth and stepped back.

He wrapped his arms around her shoulders and kissed her temple. Somehow he needed to reassure everything would be fine.

"It appears someone has beaten us," he said.

Inside was utter chaos. Empty boxes stacked haphazardly, as if someone had thrown them in a pile without care. Clothes hurled across the cement floor. A broken desk chair rested next to a cracked mirror.

Releasing her, he picked up a small metal file cabinet, set it upright, and closed the two empty drawers.

"Yes, they have." She sounded dejected.

How stupid could he be? This was hers and her dead husband's memories someone had tried to destroy. He looked at the mess again. Something was wrong with the destruction.

"They didn't find it," he said.

"What? How can you be certain?"

She picked up a shirt and started to fold the clothing as her tears fell. He grabbed her hands, stopping her futile motions and pulled her back into his arms. He wanted to protect her, find a way to help.

"The destruction looks more like someone became frustrated, not methodically looking for an object. If they were so irritated by their failure, I wonder why they didn't burn it down? That would certainly do away with any fingerprints or evidence."

"I'm glad they didn't." Her voice cracked. Then she took a shaky breath. "I hate to think of all of Vinny's things burned. Maybe like you said they didn't find it. If they had burned the building down, how would they ever be sure I can't use it against them?"

"True. They'll need to see whatever it is before they destroy it."

He rubbed his cheek in her hair. Her tension slowly drained away and she became softer, pliant in his arms.

"When are you going to tell me what is so important about the key and what it had locked up?"

She glanced up. "I really don't know what it went to. But I thought it might be in Vincent's things. Obviously, I wasn't the only one. I just know it's important evidence against his boss."

He was glad she finally admitted it to him.

"I just want this nightmare to end. I want a normal life," she muttered against his chest.

He squeezed her.

"Let's get out of here," he whispered in her ear.

"No. Let me look around. I might spot something they missed."

"All right. I really don't expect to find it here. But if you'll keep an eye out for anything you think the key would go in, I'm pretty sure I can find a way to open whatever without it." Did he sound as hopeless as she did? He looked again at the chaotic mess. "Let's divide this up. I'll take this side and you can start over there." He picked up a small sequined cloth. "Something tells me some of this isn't his."

She snatched the bikini bottom out of his hand and jammed it into the file cabinet.

"I stored my costumes and anything that just didn't fit with my new, small-town life."

He grinned and wondered if he could talk her into taking some of the costumes home and giving him a private show. His imagination and her blush brought a stiffness to his movements as he walked further into the building, skirting overturned trunks. A furtive shift of his pants brought some relief. He glanced to one side and a large, framed picture caught his attention. He shook the loose shattered glass. The woman looked familiar.

"That's Audrey Hepburn. Vinny was crazy about her," Mary said, looking over his shoulder.

"He had a framed picture of her? Almost life-sized?"

"Yep. It hung on the wall in his office at home."

"That didn't bother you?" Most wives were funny about their men having pictures of women, even if they were beautiful, fully-dressed actresses, deceased or not.

"He said he first noticed my long neck. That I had an Audrey Hepburn-type neck. How could I be jealous? She brought me and Vinny together."

He liked how she felt comfortable talking about her husband around him. He noticed how she switched from calling the man Vinny to Vincent. The formal Vincent when it had to do with work and Vinny when it was senti-mental. That was when *he felt* tinges of jealousy.

Yet he understood how talking about the dead helped a person feel their loved one's life wasn't wasted. He and his dad never talked about his mother. Too much hurt and guilt between the two of them, he guessed. But they should. His mom's life mattered.

With a shake of his head to clear it of his own nostalgic thoughts, he placed the picture against the wall and started a methodical search, like the burglar should have done, of the building, looking in, under, through anything not damaged beyond recognition.

"Oh, this is hopeless. We have no idea what the key went to and if they couldn't find it, what makes me believe we can? Despite the damage, I bet experts did this. Probably the only fingerprints are Vincent's, mine, and mom's, and now yours. Even the moving men I used had work gloves."

He looked down at the large collection of old DVDs and photo albums, all of Audrey Hepburn. Hell, the guy had been really hung up on her. Such a shame. To have Mary for a wife and be obsessed with... He shook his head. Well, he wouldn't waste his time admiring an image on a TV screen.

Chapter Twenty-Seven

fter she and Luke searched through the storage building, they headed back to the hospital.

The long ride gave Mary too much time to think.

After Luke slid behind the wheel, he'd asked which app and music she wanted and then stared straight ahead. He obviously had something on his mind too.

What was she to do now? She had only this evening and tomorrow morning. Jorge expected the evidence by eight tomorrow evening. True, chances were he had stolen the key and found what it fit. Then he would have whatever leverage she'd had to protect herself.

As they walked into her mom's room, Mary felt helpless seeing her mother looking so small in the hospital bed. She stayed all afternoon and into the evening, checking with the doctor and nurses on how her mom was responding to the treatments. They said everything looked good and pointed to a full recovery as long as her mom followed doctor's orders and worked hard in rehab. Their quick thinking of calling an ambulance and sending her to the hospital had made the difference.

While Mary visited with her mom. Luke left to run an errand in her car as he still had the spare key fob. She'd been too occupied with her worries to ask what he was up to. Fortunately, he returned moments before visiting hours were over.

Tired and beyond any need to talk, she enjoyed their companionable silence. His presence beside her was enough to help her handle all the stress.

Their steps echoed in the shadowed parking garage. She moved ahead of Luke toward her Lexus, the lone car at the opposite end of the lane from the elevators. The early fall evening was chilly especially after the over-warm hospital room. She pressed the button on her key fob that would start the engine, an accessory she appreciated on cooler nights.

It was like a giant hand slammed her against the cement block wall beside the elevator. Heat and shards of glass and metal sprayed them. Vaguely, she saw Luke sprawled nearby. His head lifted and he rolled over onto his back. Then everything went black.

Sometime later she felt someone pulling her to her feet, her ears feeling like they were stuffed with cotton. Luke. He shouted at her, but nothing registered. He pushed and prodded her down the stairs and came to a stop in the middle of a small lawn between the hospital and parking deck.

Luke had his phone to his ear, talking to someone though she couldn't make out a word.

Still unfocused, she heard the muffled sounds of alarms and sirens in the distance, and Luke talking. She understood one word. Bomb.

Oh, God. Jorge tried to kill them.

Chapter Twenty-Eight

"Mary, baby." Panic filled his voice as Luke ran his hands over her body. "Honey, please listen to me. Are you hurting anywhere? Are you okay?"

He prayed there were no serious cuts or broken bones, the impact from the explosion ringing in his ears. Glass and metal clung to her face and clothing. He was careful not to rub and embed the shards, blowing and flicking off as many as he could.

He guessed his face looked a lot liked hers, speckled with black dirt and cuts, some deeper than others. A swipe at what he thought was sweat on his upper lip revealed his nose was bleeding. Grateful no blood streamed from Mary's nose or ears, he wrapped his arms around her shaking shoulders.

Luke almost punched the doctor when she gripped his shoulder to move him out of the way in an effort to check for injuries. From all of the conversations flying around his head, he pieced together that a nurse and an orderly were also hurt in the explosion. Luckily, no one was killed. If the bomb had gone off during daylight hours, the story would be different.

Within seconds, after the doctor found them, they were surrounded by several scrubs-clad personnel forcing them onto stretchers. He wanted to protest but each time he tried to sit up the world spun faster and faster.

For the next few hours, they were x-rayed, cleaned, and stitched. He'd busted his head on the cement wall, needing six stitches and rest from the concussion.

By the time the police and the local FBI finished their questioning, Luke's patience had ended. He needed to see Mary. Finally, an orderly pushed his hospital stretcher into a large room with several curtains. As the material was pulled to one end, Luke spotted Mary. She turned and smiled at him. There were cuts across her forehead and one cheek. His heart tightened. What if she'd died? The thought was too terrible to explore.

"Some date, huh?" She laughed and held a rib.

"Broken?" If he could get his hands on the person who had set the explosive, he'd gladly break every bone in his body.

"No. Feels like it. Just bruised." Her words slurred.

"They gave you some good stuff, huh?"

"Yeah." Her loopy smile had him chuckling.

"I bet you're a happy drunk."

"How did you know?"

"Just a wild guess."

A nurse walked in, checked his chart, and then left.

"On our next date, let's skip the flying through the air, okay? I'm more a dinner and movie sort of guy."

She laughed and then groaned, holding her side. "Don't. You're a cruel man, Mr. Luke Blackwood, for making me laugh."

He wished he could take the pain from her. Instead his bad luck had brought this on her.

As he looked at her sweet face, her bottom lip began to tremble and tears welled up in her eyes.

"Oh, no, sweetheart, please don't cry. Everything'll be okay. We'll find out who did this."

She shook her head, causing her hair to slap the pillow. He worried she would hurt herself if she didn't quit. In measured movements, he slipped off the stretcher, taking the IV drip with him. He crawled onto the opposite side from her bruised rib, arranging her head to rest on his shoulder.

In no time, her racing heart slowed and her body became limp.

"I must tell you something important, Luke," she said, pronouncing each word with a slur.

"Shh, you need your sleep. You can tell me later."

"I'm so stupid."

"Shh, no, you're not. Sleep now."

"I'm afraid."

"I've got you. I won't let anyone hurt you again." He prayed he could keep that promise.

"Not me. I'm afraid for you."

He held his breath for a moment. When was the last time someone besides his dad worried about him?

After pulling the sheet up to her chin and over his chest, he caressed her shoulder.

"I'll be here when you wake." With his free hand he rubbed the center of his chest. Somehow this woman had lifted the hard knot he'd had for so long resting near his heart.

Her breath fanned across his skin.

"You're in danger staying near me. Jorge called the other

day. He is, uh, was Vincent's boss. Wanting the key." The drugs were playing with her concentration. "He has the key now. He must. If not, why kill us?"

"I figured he was the one wanting it." Her body needed rest but he sensed she wanted to voice her concerns before she fell asleep. "Why didn't you tell me about Jorge calling?"

"I hated getting you involved in my sordid life."

Moisture dripped onto his chest. She was crying again.

Scooting up to a sitting position, he pulled her closer and began to rock her in comfort. "Shh. I'm glad you did."

"I have to tell you." She wiped her face. "The key fits something that holds evidence against Jorge. Enough to send him away for a long, long time."

"Baby, you told me that already." He kissed the top of her head. "Are you certain it will protect you?"

"Vincent swore it was insurance against his boss. He never told me what it was specifically."

So that was how Mary was blackmailing Jorge. He wanted to slug Vincent in the face. Hadn't he known he signed Mary's death certificate with that key? She didn't possess a criminal mind to blackmail a mobster.

Worried she would insist on continuing her husband's crazy scheme, he cupped her face between his hands, forcing her to look into his eyes.

"Mary, you understand that you have to tell the police, the FBI, or someone who can protect you better than me."

Her cold fingers caught his hands. "No. Not the FBI. They got Vincent killed. We can't tell the police either. Telling anyone will only get you killed. Then where would I be?" Her eyes widened, pleading for his understanding.

He pulled her back into his arms. Beneath his fingers he felt light tremblers race down her body. Her fear was real.

"Okay for now." There had to be a way to keep her safe. "What do you suggest we do?"

"I don't know. Oh, God, I wish I did."

She continued crying softly while he helplessly held her. A grim determination gripped him.

Come hell or high water, he would protect her with his life.

Chapter Twenty-Nine

Early Sunday morning, Mary walked into her mom's hospital room with Luke behind her.

"Oh, my goodness, girl. What happened to you?" Her mom sat up straighter in the bed, tears welling up in her eyes.

"We're okay. Please, please don't worry." She kissed her mom on the cheek. "My car blew up but we were far enough away that we received only a few cuts and bruises."

"Oh, no. I heard the nurses talking about it, but never thought it was you." Her brow wrinkled with worry as she leaned forward to whisper, "Lazaro?"

"We believe so."

"What did the police say?"

"You know I couldn't tell them everything. All the evidence would be circumstantial anyway. Just like last time with Vincent." It was a helpless feeling knowing she couldn't tell the authorities the truth. Of course, the truth wasn't always enough to find justice.

Luke stepped closer to the bed.

"How are you doing?" he asked, patting her mom's hand.

"I swear if I eat another Jell-O cup or tasteless green bean, I'll scream. No salt means no flavor." She shook her finger at her daughter. "You get me out of here. I want to go home."

"Please. The doctors already told you and me no." Mary sat next to her mom and hugged her to her.

"I want to sleep in my own bed. Stupid little beds. If it wasn't for the stupid rails, I would fall out. Stupid hospital."

Luke chuckled.

Her mom glared at him. "What's so funny, boy?"

"The *stupid* situation?" His eyebrows rose as the older woman continued to glare.

"Just one more week." Mary rested her hand on her mom's arm. "They need to keep an eye on you and after a week of physical therapy you should get to come home."

Good thing too. Mary had enough to worry about without her mom being at home while this craziness was going on.

"Humph." Her mom crossed her arms. "No way should you be alone in that house. You need to leave. Go to a hotel somewhere in Birmingham where that asshole can't find you." The fear in her mom's eyes came back full force when she spotted Mary and Luke's bruises and cuts.

Concern for her mom—another stroke could be fatal—shook Mary as badly as the explosion.

"I'm tired of running. Everything will be okay. Luke will be there." Though they hadn't discussed anything of the sort, she knew Luke would stand by her.

The realization was comforting and a little surprising too. Fear and anxiety had filled every waking moment once Vinny started talking with the FBI. Even after his death and her escape from Vegas, she continued to dread each day and what it could bring. That was, until Luke came into her life. She felt many things for him but the two most important were protected and respected. Even Vinny, as wonderful as he had tried to be, had failed at those in the end. Would Luke do the same to her? Her intuition and her heart said no. Oh, God, she was falling in love with him.

"Don't worry. I'll keep an eye on Mary. Bubba's promised to have a patrol car drive by every hour."

Why had he involved the sheriff? She turned to glare at Luke. The last thing they needed was the police involved. They would want details she couldn't provide. She was unsure of when Jorge would attack again. Chances were he had the key. Who was to say Jorge didn't already have the evidence? And he was playing with her. Maybe he believed she knew what the evidence was and how to take him down. No. Something else was going on.

Luke's dad waited in his truck in front of the hospital. She sat between the two men and made small talk with the reverend. So many emotions churned inside her, from worry for her mom to anger at Luke's betrayal to the police. No need to upset Luke's dad by telling his son where he could take a flying leap.

The sun peeked above the farmhouse's roof when they drove up. Everything looked as they had left it until she opened the front door.

"Oh, no. No. No." Mary stepped out of the way for Luke and his dad to come in and see.

Books and furniture turned topsy-turvy. Glass sprinkled across the floors like jagged diamonds. Pictures taken from the walls and thrown across the room. Cushions and pillows slashed. Mary stumbled through the rooms unsure what to do. She should've known this would happen, especially after seeing what had been done to the storage building.

But this was so close, her personal space. A helpless feeling washed over her.

"I've called Bubba. He'll be here in a couple minutes. Dad will take you to our house," Luke said. She could tell by the look he gave her, he expected her to fall apart.

"No. I'm staying here. This is my home. I'll talk to the sheriff." Straightening her shoulders, she took a deep breath and picked up a lamp, placing it on the end table.

Then she rushed over to a large cabinet with broken glassware. Inside a bottom drawer she found her laptop untouched between a stack of tablecloths. Whoever had wrecked the place thought linens were unimportant and wouldn't make a statement or hide something valuable. Or she was plain lucky.

"Mary, you can't stay here."

"Why not?" She returned the computer to its hiding place. "They know whatever they were looking for isn't here. If they still believe I have it, they'll find me at your house. At least here, I have home-field advantage." She shoved the stuffing back into a cushion before glancing at Luke's dad. "And no one else has to be in the line of fire."

"Okay. But I'm staying with you." Luke's tone brooked no argument.

She glared at him for a moment. Was he part of this? While the men had checked the other rooms, she'd looked at the alarm. It was intact. Whoever turned it off had the code. She would call the security company and find out how to program in a new code that they wouldn't even know. A nod of her head broke their stare-down.

Her glare at Luke returned with the screaming siren and flashing blue lights coming down the drive.

"Is that really necessary?" She sighed with disgust.

"Bubba had to make sure he could get here fast enough. So yes." He shrugged.

Closing her eyes, she shook her head. Defeat crashed down on her shoulders.

Obviously, he thought the sheriff could help.

Chapter Thirty

After Bubba left, Luke and his dad helped Mary put the house into some type of order. Twice he caught her crying while holding a broken object. Considering how much she had been through the past several days, she was a strong woman to shed only a few tears.

Hours later, they had the downstairs and a couple of bedrooms upstairs looking livable. Then his dad hollered goodbye. They were finally alone.

"I'm heating up chicken and dumplings for an early lunch. Want some?"

"Yes." The kitchen had the least damage. Whoever ransacked the house had left the dishes alone.

In no time, they were eating.

A strong wind from a coming storm shook the house, magnifying the usual old sounds of creaking wood and groaning foundation.

Luke sensed Mary's tension. Each time a tree limb slapped against the house she would jump. He thought about asking her to turn on the small television in the kitchen, create some white noise as he wasn't much of a talker. Then he remembered the set had been thrown to the floor, unlikely to work.

"You never told me why you hated Chet so much." Mary scooted her chair from the table and stood.

He was aware they were ignoring how their time was ticking down, but there was nothing they could do. No key. No clue to what it would fit. They would figure something out. At least, they were still alive. Possibly, she did want to know his relationship with Chet. Certainly, listening to his problems would keep her mind off Jorge Lazaro's vendetta.

"You've never asked," he said with a touch of sass. "By the way, he hates me the same." Maybe opening up to her would help her to open up to him.

He carefully wiped his mouth with a paper napkin and pushed back in his chair.

She picked up their bowls and took them to the sink. "Well, I guess I'm asking."

"I'll tell you what. After we take showers, we can sit in front of the fireplace. I'll start the gas logs now. How about that?"

"Sounds lovely. I can make us some cocoa. You go ahead and take your shower first." She bent down and reached into a cabinet, pulling out a pot.

Luke's dick hardened as he watched her jeans stretch across her beautifully shaped ass.

"Sure," he responded without really thinking of what he was saying. "A cup of hot chocolate sounds good. I haven't had any since I was a kid."

He turned away before she caught him staring and headed toward the shower.

The steaming spray felt good on his bruised and battered body. He picked up the bottle of shampoo and sniffed. It was her honeysuckle smell. The same scent he wanted to wrap around him at night. Massaging the satiny substance into his hair, he liked the thought of having her scent on him though he preferred a different method.

A quick turn of his wrist and the water changed to cold which helped shake the increasing need to be between Mary's legs. Never a hound dog with other women, he wished he could control his impulse to think with a one-track mind, at least where Mary was concerned.

Five minutes later, he walked into the kitchen. The scent of chocolate engulfed him with memories of his mom. Shaking his head, he chased them away. Now wasn't the time.

Fascinated by her graceful movements, he watched as Mary lifted a paper towel over one cup and spilled a white substance into the liquid. She stirred and steam drifted above the rim.

A secret ingredient?

"Mary," he called out.

She jumped, covering her heart with one trembling hand. "You scared me."

"Sorry. Guilty conscience?" No sooner than he said that, he recognized the amber pharmacy bottle off to one side poorly hidden by the flour canister.

Why was she planning to knock him out?

Chapter Thirty-One

Did he know?

Mary searched his features for any sign of suspicion. She needed to meet with Jorge that evening without Luke tagging along, and there was only one way she could think of to insure that he was out of danger. Her mother's sleep medicine should do it. Instead of one tablet, two should knock out a man of his size.

While Luke had taken a shower, she'd crunched the tablets to powder and then grated chocolate on top. There would be no sign of the drug once she poured the cocoa.

Would he believe her hands trembled from the fright he gave her? *Pretend as if nothing is wrong.*

She stirred the hot milk again. She hated doing this to him. He'd been nothing but kind. There was no way around it. She refused to let her feelings interfere with her plans. Luke was the first man she'd feelings for since Vinny's death. If he went with her, he would be on Jorge's radar and could lose his life. She couldn't take the chance. Jorge's temper was unpredictable and often volatile.

She'd be safe in the diner with the usual crowd around. Right? Of course.

On a deep breath, she turned and nearly spilled the cups. He stood less than a foot away with a scowl. That wasn't good.

"What do you think you're doing?"

Had he seen what she'd done? Doing her best to keep an innocent look on her face, she held out the doctored cup.

"About to drink some delicious hot cocoa."

Good. As long as she kept to truths, at least half truths, she might get away with it. She held back a sigh. What had happened to her promise to be a good girl?

"You know what I mean, Honey," he said in a no-nonsense tone.

That wasn't good. She equaled his calling her Honey in that tone with her mom calling her Mary Katherine.

Luke grabbed her wrist and took the cup. As she watched in numb disbelief, he poured the contents into the sink. Then he took her cup and lightly placed it on the counter.

Keeping an iron grip on her arm, he pulled until her body came to rest against his.

"What did you plan to do when you had me doped up? I would be of little use if you wanted to have your way with me." The last was said with a trace of humor. She had expected anger, possibly accusations of betrayal. But humor?

She glanced at the sink before returning her attention to the man rubbing her back, causing her body to soften and relax in his arms.

Ashamed by her actions, she decided it was fate he'd caught her. Maybe it was fate that caused Vinny, a grown man, older than Luke, to die trying to protect her. Who was she to try to change whatever was to come? Jorge probably knew about Luke already.

"I wanted to protect you." She was done with lying to this man.

"Hmm. And why do you believe you need to do that?"

For whatever reason the rumble in his chest as he spoke made her feel safe. Loved. She closed her eyes, savoring the feeling.

"This evening." Her mouth became dry at the thought. "I meet with Jorge. He wants the evidence."

"What were you going to do? We haven't found it."

He'd said "we." She liked that. Since Vincent's death, she'd been alone, and now she wasn't. She felt giddy. No doubt a stupid grin was on her face.

"Meet with him and ask for more time? Maybe even bargain with him?"

He squeezed her as if she'd made a move to step away. "Bargain with what?"

Though their conversation was serious, rather deadly in fact, she couldn't stop grinning. She relished having someone worried about her. In his case, he had no idea how she handled situations like having her life threatened. Most people living a normal life would be unaware of what to expect, but after being married to Vincent, she'd lived with danger day in and day out. It hadn't been easy. Yet she knew she would do whatever it took to protect the ones she loved. She'd failed once, she refused to do so again.

"Bargain with what?" he repeated, anger creeping into his voice.

"With money," she answered.

His brows lifted in surprise.

Had he thought she would use her body? Now her temper rose

"I can't believe you thought I would…that's just sickening. Jorge is scum." She pushed and stepped out of his arms. "I don't understand you at all. For that matter, why are you helping me?"

He sat in a kitchen chair and waited for her to do the same. She eased into the spot across from him.

"I admire you," he said with a tenderness that almost broke her heart.

No one had ever said such a thing to her.

"I don't see how. I got my husband killed. I've placed my mother in danger. At the rate things are going, I might get you killed too."

"I thought you said the FBI had something to do with your husband's death."

She stood and began washing the cups. A good excuse to turn her back. He couldn't see her face.

"Mary?"

"I insisted Vincent work with them. We had a chance to live a normal life. I had no idea Jorge would find out so quickly."

Her mind raced with the terror she'd lived with during those first few days after Vincent's death. If they hadn't moved when they did, she was certain she'd be dead too.

She put up the last cup and spread the drying cloth over the side of the sink. When she turned to look at Luke, she almost crumbled from the compassion softening his face.

"Come here." He moved his chair away from the table and drew her into his lap. "You have nothing to feel guilty about."

"Ha! This coming from a man that blames himself for his mother's…" She covered her mouth. What was she thinking?

Chapter Thirty-Two

L uke felt like someone had thrown cold water over him.

"Who told you?"

"Chet?"

"You're really a terribly liar. Who have you been talking to?" He hated frightening her. Usually he didn't care what anyone thought. For that matter, he did blame himself for his mother's death.

"Does it matter? I know you blame yourself. I also know you didn't kill her."

"How are you so certain of it? You weren't there." Pain from the guilt made his tone harsher than necessary. He felt shame when her face paled and she jerked from him.

"No. Why don't you explain it to me?" She moved from his lap and took a seat across the table.

"Okay. Just remember you asked for it. The ugly truth." Her distance was for the best. He hadn't rehashed this tale for many years though the scene and events were never far from his thoughts. "I was twelve. Ma had been back home only a couple months from Bryce's, that's a psych hospital in Tuscaloosa, you know for crazy people."

"Luke," she said in a sympathetic tone.

Her hand came to rest on top of his. He made to pull away, instead found his fingers clasping hers.

"She had a problem with depression. When she returned home she looked so fragile. My ma was a beautiful woman. Men liked looking at her. It was hard being a preacher's wife, so much is expected. Every word said, every move made is examined." He closed his eyes, as seeing Mary pitying the boy he'd been would only anger him. He needed her to know his side of the story. "I had gotten suspended from school for slicing a couple bicycle tires."

"Bubba's and Chet's? Why did you do it? They were your friends then, right?"

The gossip mill in Sand City was alive and well. He could imagine the things she'd heard.

"Yeah. I had thought they were friends. But friends don't peek on a friend's mother as she takes a shower."

"Oh, no." She shook her head.

"Bubba said he didn't know Chet was looking at my ma. He claimed that he thought Chet was spying on me, to catch me in the act of...you know. We had stolen one of Chet's brother's *Playboy*s...you know how hormones are going wild at that age."

She nodded, a faint grin on her face.

"Bubba had sworn he would make it up to me the rest of his life," he said as he rubbed the soft, smooth skin on her hand. "He's always wanted to be a cop and even at twelve he knew a Peeping Tom charge would ruin his chances."

"That's why he lets you go and takes your side."

"Part of it." It was easier to tell her than he thought it

would be. "He feels guilty about my ma dying too. He knows he's partly to blame."

"I don't understand. She had a stroke. That can't be anybody's fault."

Feeling restless, he released his hold on her hand and stood, pacing across the kitchen floor.

"Ma was waiting for me when I came in from school. They had called ahead and told her I had been suspended for fighting. She was upset and angry. I don't blame her. She didn't know why I'd done it and I refused to tell her. We argued about why I wouldn't explain. How could I tell her that my friends had turned out to be perverts?"

Every moment burnt in his memory came back to him. He'd acted like a selfish jerk to his ma. He'd resented her being gone during Christmas. He resented how being in that hospital had given the town so much to gossip about her.

"I said some hateful, hurtful things to her. I'll always be ashamed of the way I acted. She didn't deserve such treatment from me," he said, his voice husky with sorrow.

He wished over and over again he could take back the words. Anything for her to forgive him, to tell her one last time that he loved her and he was so sorry.

When his mom had stumbled, appearing to have difficulty breathing, he never imagined she was having a stroke. Then her face whitened and she crumpled to the floor before he could catch her. The EMTs said she was probably dead before her head connected with the coffee table.

She'd been a beautiful woman and too sweet for this world. No history of a heart condition.

"So she had the stroke during the argument?"

"Yeah." He braced his hands on the kitchen counter, his head hanging between his shoulders. A wash of pain and coldness flowed over him. The unexpected comfort of Mary's arms coming around his waist and her warm body pressing against his back returned him to the present.

"That's a horrible thing for a twelve-year-old boy to go through."

"I didn't tell you so you can pity me," he said, his voice hoarse from the sadness gripping him.

"I pity the boy that lost his mother at an important time in his life when he needed her the most. But I don't pity the man. You've grown up to be someone that knows he's made mistakes. You might still be feeling your way, but I see a man pulling himself together little by little, the way any well-built house is put together. That's the same for any good person. A person that helped me in ways I cannot count."

He clasped her wrist and pulled her around between him and the counter. She looked at him with such tenderness. He never expected a woman who knew the truth to understand. Unable to find his voice, embarrassed by the special way she made him feel, he merely stared at her as his chest swelled with pride and love for this woman.

She tilted her head and caressed his cheek. "Since I've never seen you start a fight, I can only guess Chet feels guilty but refuses to acknowledge his part in all of it." Her eyes widened. "He's the only person you fight with." She chuckled. "Well, that is, when you're not attacking that handsome devil, Evil. I have to agree they both deserve a beating. Evil needs to learn to shut his mouth."

He didn't like to think of Mary checking out Evil.

"Enough about those two and the past. Let's talk about how much money you believe will encourage Jorge to bargain?" When she said the amount, he whistled. "Do you have that much money?"

"That and a whole lot more. I'm very talented with investments." She blushed.

His dick hardened. There was nothing sexier than a smart woman with a blush to her cheeks.

He shut his eyes for a split moment to focus his concentration on what was important. Protecting Mary and getting ready for that evening. Somehow he would make sure that SOB ended up in jail. Between her dead husband endangering her by having her hold onto blackmail information and the ex-boss placing Mary's life in danger by blowing up her car, she needed someone looking after her interests and not their own.

And he was that person.

Chapter Thirty-Three

Mary wanted to make love with Luke again. All signs of the bad boy had been replaced with the strong and compassionate man standing before her.

She had other things to tell him but nothing so important that would be worth waiting to jump his bones. He apparently guessed by her grin what she was thinking as his eyes lit up in anticipation.

As she wrapped her arms around his neck and lifted to her tiptoes to kiss him, someone knocked on the door. His mouth took hers before the knocking became insistent.

She sighed when he cursed and placed her from him. Happy to have time to straighten her clothes and regain her composure, she came up behind Luke at the front door. From his tone she could tell he'd rather slam the door in the visitor's face. Evil. His name was certainly an indication of what she felt at the moment.

"You can tell me tomorrow. I'm kinda busy," Luke said in exasperation and started to close the door on the man.

Dressed in his usual dirty jeans and T-shirt, Evil filled

the doorway, hands holding opposite sides of the frame, preventing Luke from following through with his initial reaction.

"I swear it won't take but a moment." Evil looked around Luke's shoulder. "Mary." He nodded at her and returned his attention to Luke. "Come on, man, I wouldn't bother you if I didn't think it was important. I could've just called."

"Yeah, why didn't you?" Luke asked, grinding out the last word.

"I don't think Mary's landline is safe and you know how I feel about cell phones. All that info floating through the air. Anyone can pick up on that."

"You're a paranoid SOB." With a push of the door, Luke sighed. "Come in and make it quick."

"Thanks, man. It's getting cold out there." Evil stepped inside, rubbing his arms as he looked at Mary, obviously waiting for her to leave.

Luke closed the door and stepped over to her.

But something about what he said didn't ring right. A nagging feeling froze her to the spot. Whatever he wanted to tell Luke, she needed to hear it.

"Mary, can you give us a moment?" Luke picked up her hand and kissed her fingers.

She faltered for a second, wanting to give in like so many times she did to Vincent. "No. I want to hear what Evil has to say." Standing firm, she held his gaze.

"Okay." Luke nodded, her hand still in his as he turned to Evil. "She's got a right to know whatever you found out."

Evil shifted his jaw as he studied her. "All right." His dark countenance made clear why he was called Evil. With such dark looks and the aura of danger around him, she became chilled by his presence alone.

Unsure if she'd shivered or he'd noticed the chill bumps on her arms, she was glad Luke placed an arm around her shoulders and pulled her to his warm body.

The look Evil gave them nudged her closer to Luke. She had no idea why he didn't like her. Unless he thought with her background that she was playing a dangerous game with his friend.

"We're waiting," Luke pressed.

She liked the way Luke's fingers played with the skin of her arm, the tension easing out of her body as another more pleasant tension took over. Why couldn't she stand near the man without thinking about sex? Now wasn't the time. She placed her hand over his.

Evil opened his mouth and stopped when someone knocked on the door. "That's Smooth now. He might have more intel for us."

Mary looked at Luke. Hadn't he noticed the catchword? There was more to Evil than met the eye. She hadn't forgotten he'd dug up more information about her than most thugs would ever manage. He needed watching.

A cool gust of wind came in with Smooth. The younger Rogan was better looking than his darker brother if a person liked the fair-haired-boy-next-door look. Freckles lightly sprinkled across his face framed blueish-green eyes and well-defined lips. His stubby blond lashes kept his face from being feminine and if that wasn't enough, the broad shoulders certainly indicated male strength.

"You're just in time. I was about to tell them what you told me. Did you find out anything more?" Evil slapped his brother on the back.

Smooth shook his head.

"You want to tell them?" Evil asked.

The younger man shook his head again.

Chapter Thirty-Four

"Dammit, Evil, tell us. This mysterious shit is for the birds." Luke had waited for a fraction of a second longer before he'd had enough.

When Mary moved from under Luke's arm, he reached for her.

She shook her head as she grabbed his hand and walked to the couch. "Let's all sit. We'll be a little more comfortable."

Luke pulled her next to him. The thought of her being out of reach for even a few minutes, after yesterday's near-miss, was not an option. Smooth and Evil took the over-stuffed chairs facing the couch.

The light-haired brother leaned back and crossed his legs, ankle on knee. Evil sat on the edge as if on guard from an attack.

"Smooth overheard Bubba talking with someone on his cell phone. He was calming the person down. Whoever it was, they were upset about a gambling debt they owed. The bookie was making noise about getting paid." Evil spread his legs, forearms on his knees as he looked down at his clasped hands.

"Nothing unusual about that. Bubba has told me that people complain to the local sheriff about some of the dumbest things. Half of this town bets on football games. Hell, they stand around and bet on how many times I can hit Chet before he goes down." Luke shook his head in disgust from his own part played, and others egging him on so they could win a bet. "Do you have any idea who it is?"

"No. But he also said that the person shouldn't worry. That he knew how to take care of the guy," Evil said.

That was odd. Bubba normally listened and then brushed off stuff like that.

"Where was Bubba when you overheard this conversation?" Luke asked when he turned to Smooth.

It was so strange how the brothers always knew more than the gossips of what was going on in town. Like they were often in the right place at the right time, or wrong place at the right time. All depending on a person's point of view.

"Outside the sheriff's office." The younger brother sniffed and then scratched at the tip of his nose, staring off at the decorative fireplace mantel.

Luke grappled with the possibilities: Chet, or one of the deputies or their families became entangled in professional gambling or a big time bookie? Then an old conversation came to mind. "Didn't I hear at one time that Susan grew up in New Jersey?"

Mary tilted her head. "Yes and no. She attended a cooking school in New York but stayed with an uncle in Jersey during the time." She frowned. "What are you getting at?"

He understood the concern about her friend. Yet they

needed to consider everyone as a suspect. He rubbed the back of his neck.

As unlikely for Bubba to be involved with just anyone's gambling debts, Luke had a bad feeling about Mary's husband's strange fascination with a decades-dead actress, even with her ethereal beauty. Fuck, look at Mary. She was ten times as beautiful. Of course, he was a bit biased since he'd fallen for her.

Maybe he was going off the deep end, but there was something strange about a big tough guy owning that picture. Plus it didn't go with his decor. Yeah, he knew it was strange to notice, but he'd been interested in everything about Mary's dead husband.

He turned to Evil.

"Did you bring that picture I asked you to hold for me?" He would never understand what made him decide to call Evil to meet him in Birmingham and have him—of all people—take the picture off his hands for safe keeping until he returned to Sand City, but a good thing he had. Otherwise, the picture would be ashes or sliced up or even stolen.

"Yeah, it's in the truck."

"Hand me your keys and I'll get it."

Evil tossed his truck keys to Luke. No one said a word while he walked outside and returned carrying the framed picture of Audrey Hepburn.

"While you were visiting with your mom yesterday, I went back to the storage shed. Something kept bugging me about that framed picture." He turned the picture, plied apart the already cracked frame, and then peeled the torn backing away. Two one-inch-thick rolls of papers fell into his hands. "The heavy frame seemed out of place with all of the ultra-modern shit Vincent had owned in his office."

"Is it what we've been looking for?" Mary asked.

"Not exactly. I haven't read everything, but they might give us a clue to where the evidence is hidden. There's a list of Lazaro's properties. He owns a large percentage of a casino in Atlantic City." He unrolled them and handed several sheets to Mary.

Smiling, she looked as if he'd given her a million dollars. "Let's take this to the police."

He really hated to burst her bubble.

"No. None of the information is illegal." Unrolling the second set, he handed her a sheet with columns. Mary passed the sheets she'd already examined to Evil and Smooth to look over. "This sheet has a column of initials and two columns of numbers."

"Man, why bring the whole fucking picture?" Smooth laughed as if he thought Luke was an idiot.

What an asshole.

"Because I wanted everyone to be a witness of where it was stashed. I wanted no doubt that it came from the frame." He'd learned after his time in prison people easily thought the worst of him. It was important his friends and the woman he loved had no doubts.

Mary rubbing his shoulder accompanied by her sweet look assured him she believed him.

Evil moved to the couch next to Mary, sitting on the opposite side of Luke. "If I were to guess, it looks like a bookie's VIP list and their double action." Evil shook his head. "Damn, those are some big numbers."

Luke agreed. Most of the columns had five figures, a few six. He'd seen families destroyed by this type of addiction, just the same as a drug or alcohol.

He caught Mary's frown as she looked at the numbers.

"Mary, double action is when someone places a bet and if it wins, another bet is placed using the second amount. If the first bet loses, all is lost. It can add up quickly either way. Most times, not good."

"Yeah, yeah," she said, lifting a hand as if to wave him away, without looking in his direction.

She continued to thumb through the other pages. It was obvious she was only half listening. He mentally slapped his forehead.

"Sorry. I forgot for a moment you lived and worked in Vegas."

"That's okay." Her half-grin revealed she understood he was only trying to keep everything clear. "One thing about living in Sin City, you learn all the ways a person can lose money. I never was interested in gambling. Worked too hard for my money to throw it away on an off-chance of hitting it rich."

"The initials could be anybody." Evil handed some of the sheets to his brother.

"There are only one set of initials showing as SR. They could be Susan Reed's. Actually could be any number of people." Luke placed his hand on Mary's knee when she flinched. He understood her concern about her friend.

Smooth glanced at the columns. "I don't think this is double action. I believe the first column of numbers is what they owe and then the last column is what they've paid so far. Look at this last page at the bottom." He gave the sheets back to Luke.

When Luke held the page beneath the lamp on the end table, squinting, he read the faded words. "'Total amount due.'"

Damn it. Why hadn't he caught that? True, the printing appeared to be on thin thermal paper, easy to fade or darken to the point of being unreadable. The type of paper used in old fax machines. Who used faxes nowadays? He was grateful the storage shed had been climate controlled.

"Did you check the rest of the frame?" Mary asked.

"Yeah. Nothing." He began rolling up the sheets.

Evil and Smooth stood, heading toward the door, while Luke and Mary followed close behind.

"We'll let you know if we hear anything else," Evil said before jumping into his truck. Smooth remained quiet and slid into his Shelby Mustang.

Luke couldn't help but think it was a rather nice car for a dude who did only odd jobs around town. Their side business in Birmingham must be paying off. Luke watched until the red tail lights blinked out.

"What do you think? Do you think Susan's involved with Jorge?" she asked, worry wrinkling her forehead.

Whenever Mary looked at him like that, he wanted to tell her anything to keep her smiling. He wasn't sure he could this time.

"We have a couple hours. Let's take a nap," he said instead.

Chapter Thirty-Five

Mary placed the last dish in the cabinet as Luke tossed the drying cloth into the laundry room. He'd unbuttoned his shirt a little more than usual, showing off chest hair, and rolled up his sleeves due to the heat from the stove and dishwater. The line noticeable between his pecs and the well-defined muscles on his forearms pointed to a man not afraid of physical labor. Unlike Vinny who had preferred working out with weights to achieve the strength he needed to protect himself.

She hated comparing her husband to Luke but the differences were so unique. Vinny could be as romantic as Luke, yet rarely helped in the kitchen or the house. Luke pitched in and helped to cook and clean up after they had eaten without a thought. Probably a lot to do with living in a household without a woman for so long. Then Luke was like Vincent as he wasn't afraid to stand up to bullies and knew how to handle himself in a fight. Though Luke had a vulnerable side he allowed her to see. Vincent had thought showing her a soft side meant he wasn't a true man. If only he'd known that was a true sign of a real man. As unfair as it was to compare the two, she understood part of it came from being married to Vinny for over three years. She couldn't pretend the prior years meant nothing.

She picked up her phone and called her mom. She watched Luke as he set the security alarm. Giving Luke the code may prove to be a foolish move on her part, as foolish as giving her heart. Was she setting up another heartbreak by another bad boy?

He checked the kitchen door. When he walked toward the front door, she kept her eyes on his faded-blue-jeans-covered backside. Trust him or not, she liked the way he moved. A swagger owned by any cowboy worth his salt with a six-shooter on each hip. How would he look with a black hat pulled low, shading his eyes?

After twenty minutes of her mom complaining about the food and the nurses with Mary barely listening, she disconnected the call and looked up as he stopped in front of her.

"You keep checking me out like that, you'll find yourself face first over that table with your jeans and panties around your ankles and me covering your gorgeous round bottom." His tone dared her to keep looking. "We need to rest and you're making it hard to keep my mind on that nap."

Heat swirled over her face, across her breasts, and gathered in her lower abdomen. When he'd said *making it hard*, she couldn't resist looking down at his groin. Her mouth went dry as a pine cone. She wanted to say yes, yes! If only she didn't need to talk with him about what had happened with Evil and Smooth. She had a feeling if they started making love now, she wouldn't be finished with him until tomorrow morning.

No. She had to get a grip on her baser needs. That evening she would meet with Jorge. They needed to plan a strategy. If anything happened to Luke or her mom, she could never live with herself. It was imperative they examine all their possibilities.

Geez, denying herself the pleasure of cupping that rear even for a few minutes was tearing her apart.

She cleared her throat. "As tempting as your offer is, we've got to talk."

The crooked grin he gave her said he would listen, but he planned to tempt her with more than an offer.

Since she'd received Jorge's call, her life was speeding by like a stock car on the Talladega Speedway. In many ways Luke was a stranger, yet willing to risk his life and freedom to help her. Sure, they'd already had sex. Great, mind-blowing sex for that matter. Despite that, there was so much more for her to learn about him.

"So talk." He grasped her hips, his erection felt so good, rubbing up and down at the perfect spot. "Be sure to talk dirty to me," he teased.

She really should stop him. Goodness, the man knew how to move and how to exert the right pressure.

"You're not playing fair."

He reached around her, turning a knob on the wall, dimming the kitchen lights.

"I thought it was very fair. You get to talk and I get to touch you," he said in a whisper and leaned down, kissing her neck.

"But I'm having a hard time concentrating."

"Oddly enough, me too." His warm breath tickled her neck. He thrust against her to emphasize his meaning.

The last thing she wanted to do was talk about her suspicions when each stroke of his hand heated her skin to a fevered pitch. "Lu-Luke." She swallowed. "Did you catch how Evil said 'intel.' That sounded like a cop. Or maybe military. Was he in the Army? What about the pricey car his brother owns? Do they even have a job?"

His hands slid up her sides and cupped her breasts. "Honey, the last thing I want to talk about is Evil and his brother's car. Do you have any idea what I want to do to you?" He bit her earlobe and whispered such arousing words, she was certain she would flare up like a New Year's firecracker.

"Luke. Please." Each touch of his callused, strong hands brought a sigh from her lips.

"That's it. Beg me. Plead for what I can give you, Honey."

She loved his voice. Even though she'd asked him not to call her by her stage name, when he said it in that husky, breathless way, he could call her George and it would heat her blood. With a push from her, the back of his legs was stopped by the solid-oak kitchen table. Remembering what he'd said earlier, she grabbed the end of his T-shirt and pulled up until he helped by raising his arms. A light sprinkling of dark hairs tickled her palms as she skimmed over the broad muscled expanse of his chest. His dark eyes blazed with a sensuous passion.

She began to sway as she worked her way down, humming a tune she loved to dance to when she lived in Vegas. In seconds, she'd stripped his jeans and underwear off, tossing them to the side, his feet still bare after the shower.

"Hey, isn't it time for you to strip too?" he asked with a trace of taunting.

Naked and grinning, he waited for her with his hands pressed on the table behind him and his hips thrust slightly forward. Yes, he looked better than any of the male dancers she'd known. And he wouldn't have a need for extra socks to stuff in his pants. Men and their egos. She grinned.

So he thought he had the upper hand? She began humming again and reached for the hem of her pullover blouse.

"I'm glad you like what you see." Luke had a matching smile, wicked and salacious.

Chapter Thirty-Six

Luke worked at retaining control of his body or he might pass out from the lack of blood in the upper half of his body. Watching Mary bump and grind as she stripped out of her blouse and start on her jeans had him so hard he prayed he wouldn't embarrass himself by exploding before he touched her.

His hands remained rooted to the table, afraid to move. Was he dreaming?

With each inch revealed, his skin tightened, waiting for the right moment to take what was his. She belonged to him. He may not deserve her, but every minute they spent together, he needed her more and refused to give her up.

The tune she hummed vibrated through his body, each beat magnified with the sway of her hips.

When only the scrap of silk covering her femininity remained and her thumbs slipped through the thin strips at the sides, he grabbed her. The thong landed on the floor and he twisted, stretching her across the table.

"I'm hungry again." He opened her to his gaze and

licked the tight center of the woman he was falling in love with. Taking all the time he needed to show her how much she meant to him, he stroked with his tongue and fingers until her body shook in satisfaction.

When he stood to thrust into her warmth, she sat up and placed a palm on his sternum.

"No. I have a fantasy." She gave him a coy look.

Fuck. "You're going to kill me," he said breathlessly.

He was at her mercy. When she moved off the table and pushed, his shoulders landed flat on the surface, his long legs dangling off the edge. He wanted to slow her down. Damn it, they needed to rest before meeting that asshole. Though truth be known, he would do without sleep anytime to taste Mary again and certainly do whatever she planned.

When he heard the chair scrape along the floor, he widened his eyes. She'd hooked her foot in a chair and slid it between his legs. Her gaze was savoring the sight of his hard, long dick. She enthusiastically examined and stroked it. His pulsating dick matched the beat of his heart, especially when she kneeled on the seat and took him between her lips.

He gasped and pressed the back of his head into the table beneath him, trying not to gag her by thrusting in her hot mouth.

The cool tips of her shoulder-length hair brushed his hips as she swirled the strands across his hot skin. It felt so damn good. She cupped and massaged his balls as she sucked and licked his stiff -as-a-steel-rod dick.

"You have a beautiful cock. I could play with it all day long," she said, her breath teasing his sensitive tip.

Her mouth covered him again and she drew hard on the head. He groaned in pleasure.

"Fuck, Mary. Mary, Mary, Mary."

"I like hearing you say my name. Let's see how it sounds when you scream." Her husky voice brought a surge of blood to his dick and he was sure he would blow apart.

She wrapped both hands around his hardness, squeezing tight and rotating her wrists just like he did for himself in the shower. He was thankful for her skills.

"Mary," he shouted.

He tried to hold back, but she wouldn't have any of that. One wet finger circled his anus.

"Argh, fuck."

"Uh-huh, that's not my name." She drew back and released him.

"Mary, you'll regret pushing me."

With a roar, he sat up and clasped her shoulders, tossing her face first onto the table. Her head rested on her arms as her plump rear lifted. He plunged into her slick, welcoming sheath.

"Yes." She hissed the word. "I love it. Strong and force-ful. So sexy when you lose control." Inhaling deeply, she closed her eyes. "Tomorrow I'll probably be sporting bruises. So worth it. Don't treat me like spun glass ever again. I like knowing a real man is fucking me." What was with her? She never talked this much during sex. For some reason she wanted him to know now, not later, how she felt.

The table squeaked in rhythm to his powerful thrusts. Damn, she felt so good. She released a long moan.

"Am I hurting you?" He stopped and began to move out of her.

She grasped his wrists.

"No. I swear, Luke, if you leave me like this, you'll leave this house as a eunuch." He chuckled and she squirmed, lifting her hips in encouragement to start thrusting once more.

"Eunuch, huh? Baby, we can't have that. I wouldn't be able to do this." A nudge of his hips from one side to the other brought a delighted whimper from her lips. Then he showed her how hard a real man could fuck.

Chapter Thirty-Seven

Mary watched the curtains darken with the setting sun and listened to Luke's steady breathing. Sometime in the early afternoon hours, they had managed the stairs, laughing and tripping in their sated state, finally stumbling into her bedroom and onto her queen-size bed for a nap.

Her eyes shifted to the man sleeping beside her. He'd kicked off the sheets, every delightful inch of him revealed lean muscles. Every inch had varying degrees of tan and lighter skin, showing he was a man that thought nothing of doing outdoor physical labor. She especially liked looking at how his torso met his hips, the manly grooves had her nearly drooling.

Like any woman in bed with a new lover, she found her gaze focused on his cock that had provided her with so much pleasure last night. She sensed she'd been caught staring when it began straightening and lengthening.

"You know you can touch it."

Startled, she looked up, his eyes twinkling in amusement.

"I would love to but…"

"We slept too long," he said, finishing her sentence. He sounded so forlorn, she couldn't hold back a giggle. "There you go, making fun of me," he said.

"No. No." The shadows normally around his eyes were gone. He looked happy and relaxed. Until now, she hadn't realized how tightly wound Luke was around people. Even her. "I'll do my best to make it up to you tonight."

"Tonight?"

Was she wrong to assume he would stay with her another night? Would she still be alive?

Her meeting with Jorge was in less than two hours, and she still needed to get ready and double-check on her mom. He had his own parent to check on and help, plus the work he did for her around the farm wasn't his only job. He probably needed to call others.

Her cheeks warmed with the thought of what type of work he'd been performing lately. Then a horrible notion came to her mind: was he in bed with her because she paid him? How many times had she seen other girls in the dance line sleep with bosses they feared would fire them?

She mentally shook her head. Luke wasn't afraid of her. How silly could she be? The way he responded to her touch, it wasn't from fear or some crazy idea he owed her.

If anything, she owed him. He'd retrieved the box for her. He helped keep her sane while following the ambulance with her mom inside. He was doing everything humanly possible to find the evidence that she needed to hand over to Jorge.

Evidence. She still didn't have the evidence. Her once-relaxed body tensed again.

"What's the matter?"

She should've realized Luke would pick up on her surge of anxiety.

"What am I going to tell Jorge?"

Luke pulled her into his arms. "If he has the key or the evidence, he won't show. If he does show, we'll have to think of something to say, something that would slow him down, give us a little more time."

"We'll tell him the truth. Someone stole it."

"Do you think he'll believe us?"

"No. I doubt he knows I'm a terrible liar."

"I know." His grin had her forgetting the worries about the meeting.

His lips brushed her neck. With that, her body heated and became limber, molding to his.

"I hope you're right." A tingling sparked in the center of her body. She turned in his arms and kissed him, enjoying the way he used his tongue and teeth.

She pulled her head back, looking into his lust-filled dark eyes. "You know, I do believe we have a little more time," she said as she pushed him back and straddled his hips.

"We do?" His dimpled bad-boy grin sped up her heartbeat.

She nodded. "Yeah. Taking a shower together might save at least fifteen minutes."

"Your shower large enough?" he asked.

"Oh, I think we can find a way."

He chuckled as he lifted her, her legs clasped around his waist. "I'll make sure of it."

Her head rested on his shoulder as she held on tight. She never thought she would fall in love with another bad boy, but she had. Only he'd proven himself to be a good man.

<<<>>>

Mary silently sighed as she replayed the wonderful shower she'd shared with Luke. The man was amazing. He'd lasted longer than the heated water. She snorted and, grinning like a fool, glanced at Luke as she shook her head, not wanting to confess her thoughts.

They were seated beside each other in a booth at Bill's Diner waiting for Jorge to show up. Either he was late or he had arrived and left. She was hoping for the former. Otherwise, he would bring in reinforcements and her death would be immediate.

She should be nervous, actually scared spitless. But Luke's presence helped, his calm manner contagious to the point she could easily ignore Susan's glares.

When Jorge walked into the diner, she wiped a palm on her pant leg and clasped Luke's hand.

Handsome with his dark hair and golden tan, Jorge Lazaro attracted attention from several customers, especially the women. At one time, he even drew her regard. She wouldn't think of it at this time. But she had to admit the expensive gray silk suit and costly loafers added to his allure. Jorge was never known as a conservative in how he spent his money or dressed.

"I guess this means he didn't steal the key," she murmured to Luke.

Jorge's bodyguards stood outside in their own designer suits and sunglasses, looking like two sleek wolves in the middle of a flock of sheep. A couple of patrons walked out of the diner's door and anxiously scooted around them.

While watching Vincent's former boss weave his way around the patrons, Mary fought to remain calm. He was a snake in a garden.

"Good to see you, Honey." Jorge examined her as if she sat naked and waited for his pleasure. Nothing unusual, as he treated most women to the same leer, but Luke would be unaware of that. Then Jorge looked pointedly at Luke as he slid onto the vacant seat facing them.

Before Mary could introduce the men to each other, Luke leaned forward. "You're not going to get away with it, and it's Mrs. Hightower to you."

"So that's what she's calling herself," Jorge scoffed. "Vincent always treated her like a damsel with long hair in a tower. Hell, I understood why he felt that way."

The look he gave her was a leer but a little more. Did the man feel affection for her? Yuck.

Luke grabbed Jorge's shirt in one fist and she gasped. The last thing they needed was for Jorge's bodyguards to shoot up the diner.

"Luke," she whispered. "Let him go. This isn't the place." Seconds passed before he released Jorge. "He's not worth the trouble," she added.

She stifled the urge to call Jorge several ugly names. What purpose would it serve? It would cause them more trouble.

Jorge coolly swiped at the wrinkles left by Luke's grip. As he attended to his offended wardrobe, Mary caught, out of the corner of her eye, Susan's odd reaction to Jorge's presence. Instead of making her way over to meet a stranger, Susan took two steps back and then ducked into the kitchen as if she wanted to avoid him.

"You can call yourself Mary Poppins as far as I care. I want the evidence Vincent gave you. It's only in his loving memory I haven't killed you."

The sneer on his face needed to be wiped off and Mary wished she had a way to do it. That was, a better way than telling him they didn't have the evidence nor the key. She was afraid it would also push him over the edge.

"Then why did you blow up Mary's car?" Luke asked.

She kicked Luke but he ignored her and continued to glare at the man as his hand landed on her knee and squeezed.

Vincent's former boss sat up straighter, his forehead wrinkled. "That was your car?"

Considering the local news was having a field day about the explosion, everyone knew about her car. Her very expensive fake ID had held under their scrutiny and that was the only reason she hadn't been arrested by the FBI.

"So you want me to believe you didn't have anything to do with it?" Mary's awareness of Jorge's skill as a liar had her doubting his concern.

"Now, Honey, you know better than that. Would I take a chance on you getting blown up and then some lawyer or friend," he said, looking pointedly at Luke, "turns in the evidence to the local authorities?" With his wide-eyed expression, Jorge could be very convincing.

"You would if you already have the evidence," she bluntly said.

Luke squeezed her leg again. Was he trying to tell her he approved or wanted her to be careful? Either way, she'd be bruised at this rate. So she clasped his hand and dug her nails into his palm in warning. One thing was for sure. If she wanted a truthful answer from Jorge, the only way to get it was to be upfront. Maybe she was being naïve, but she had to try.

Jorge stared at her, his beady eyes trying to see through her game. That was what all this was to Jorge.

Whoa. She hadn't realized how much more she'd learned from Vincent about the man sitting across from her. Vincent rarely talked about the work he did for Jorge, but he often talked about the man he worked for.

"You're saying you don't have the evidence?" His handsome face showed nothing, from a false friendly expression to stone cold was not a good sign.

"That's what she's saying." Luke turned his hand and clasped hers back.

She'd forgotten how nice it was to have a man who was willing to protect her. Though Vincent hadn't been the perfect husband, as he'd always looked for the excitement only dangerous men could find, he made sure she was protected and taken care of.

Jorge leaned over the table. "Then I suggest you find it. You have forty-eight hours. And that's me being kind to an ex-friend's widow. Just remember my benevolence only goes so far. As Vincent found out."

Mary grabbed Luke's arm as he started over the table after Jorge. Thankfully, her touch brought him back to his senses. No way had they needed any more attention than they were getting from the patrons in the diner.

With a short huff of humor, Jorge rose and headed toward the door.

"I'm sorry. The asshole needed his face mashed in." Luke turned to her, worry written across his face. "Do you believe he's telling the truth?"

"About not having the evidence?" she asked.

Luke nodded.

"I'm not sure. But what purpose would it serve for him to pretend he doesn't have it?"

She watched as Jorge reached his bodyguards, and with a jerk of his chin, they followed. Less than a minute later, the limo pulled away from the curb, and the small crowd on the sidewalk checking out the limo dispersed.

That was close. She'd been afraid Jorge would send them in to ensure she'd gotten the point.

A chill coated Mary's skin. The word "afraid" didn't fully describe how she felt. She knew better than anyone how dangerous Jorge could be, especially when his back was against the wall.

"Don't worry. We'll find the evidence." Luke placed his arm around her shoulders and pulled her into his warmth.

She wanted to stay and let him take care of it all, but she couldn't. He would end up dead like Vincent.

"Luke," she said in a whisper.

He leaned down, smiling. "Yes?"

How could she do this to him? She eased back toward the wall, giving him space.

"I need you to walk away." She hoped she wouldn't have to beg. Though her heart was breaking, she kept her back straight and her face emotionless, staring straight into his eyes. As she'd pointed out to him earlier, she wasn't a good liar, but this was so important she knew she could do it.

"This is not the time. You need me more than ever." His face flushed in anger and hurt.

"I know that Jorge has a weakness for me, and if you're not around, I can talk him into more time. You're just getting in the way." She swallowed hard to keep her lunch down.

"He touches you and I'll—"

"You won't do anything. You're walking away." What would she do if he called her bluff?

They continued to stare at each other until Luke gave in.

"Okay. I'll leave. But don't think this is over." He slipped out of the booth with a scary scowl and then he walked away.

She kept her face emotionless as she watched him stroll down the street until he turned the corner and out of sight. Then she crumpled, hiding her face in folded arms on the table.

What now?

She refused to cry. It was for the best. The only way to protect him. No way could she lose another man she loved.

Chapter Thirty-Eight

Luke jerked open the bar's door, wishing the handle was Jorge's neck. Blaming the slick thug for Mary's decision was as productive as slamming his hand in the door. Ten times. He knew who to blame. Vincent Dead-as-a-Doornail Hightower a.k.a. Hayden. The man hadn't treated Mary right, no matter what she thought. As soon as they had married, if Vincent had had any sense, he should've taken her far away from that slime-ball Lazaro, protecting her like a real man.

That was what Luke should do. Grab Mary and head for the hills. Yeah, she'd really love that. The woman wasn't a coward, and was well aware she would never escape Lazaro. But he needed to find someway to protect her, even from herself.

So what was he doing at the Sandbox?

Letting Mary cool off. He wearily sighed. Her and her crazy idea of protecting him from Jorge. If he wasn't so worried about her, he would shout for joy. The only reason a good woman like Mary lied was that she obviously had feelings for him, just wouldn't admit it yet. And he would make sure she admitted it and soon. For now, he felt she would be safe enough until Jorge realized they had no way of finding the evidence. That should happen about the time his extension ended.

He hesitated near the long bar then heard Evil's whistle. Everyone groaned and hollered at the idiot. The man whistled louder than anyone in Sand City, if not in the state of Alabama.

"Yo, Lu, over here."

"Fuck, man, I think my ears are bleeding now."

Luke placed a finger in each ear and shook his head, clearing it of the ringing.

"And you call yourself a preacher's son." Evil laughed.

"We have the reputation of troublemakers, not the angels our dads had hoped." Luke grinned back, reaching out to shake his friend's hand as he stopped at the pool tables in the back. Though Mary suspected Evil and Smooth of being more than what they seemed, they'd always protected his back, unlike his old friends.

Thinking of old friends...Bubba walked in and scooted up to the bar. Everyone turned to stare. They rarely ever saw him out of uniform and just as rarely inside the Sandbox, unless it was to break up a fight. He usually took Susan to the Top Hat on the other side of town.

As Luke started toward Bubba, Smooth walked out of the men's restroom and greeted the sheriff, taking the barstool beside him. Smooth leaned toward Bubba and began talking as the man nodded his head.

Smooth doing all the talking? That stopped Luke in his tracks.

Evil came up beside Luke and they both stared.

"What do you make of that?" Luke asked.

"You know my brother. He's got his secrets. Like all of us." Evil said the last in a low voice.

Surprised that Evil admitted the possibility, Luke looked at the older brother. "What's your secret?"

"Why, I'm freaking Spiderman underneath this T-shirt and jeans." He laughed and slapped Luke on the back. The loud laughter pulled Bubba and Smooth's attention to their presence. Obviously, Evil's intention.

Evil walked over to his brother. "Hey, man, you two look like you're up to no good."

Bubba jumped, his face as red as his eyes. At the same time, Smooth handled their interruption with a calmness that explained his nickname.

"Smooth's consoling me." The man wiped his nose with his sleeve and looked away.

Luke wanted to ignore the whole sordid scene but he remembered Mary pointing out that Bubba had been a kid and realized he'd done wrong. For years, he'd tried to make it up to Luke. It was time to let the past go.

"Your mom and dad okay?" Luke asked.

All three men stared at Luke. What had they expected? That he would kick a man while he was down? That was Chet's M.O., not his.

"Yeah, they're okay. It's Susan. She's returning to New Jersey and..." His voice cracked before he could finish.

"Leaving Sand City?" Evil asked.

Bubba nodded, his head hanging as he sniffled.

The men surrounding the weeping sheriff looked away, suddenly interested in the small-screen television located in the upper corner of the bar. The front door opened as two regulars decided to make their escape while a few others pulled partners onto the dance floor where last night's peanut shells scattered beneath their feet.

Then it hit Luke. This could be him if Mary left because of Lazaro's threats. Damn. She could be packing to make her getaway while he messed with these clowns.

As he turned to leave, curiosity got the best of him. "Why is Susan leaving?" The woman had helped her brother make a success of the diner and had acted as if she liked small-town life.

Bubba glanced at Smooth.

What the...? Luke couldn't believe what he was seeing. This was beyond strange. Bubba and Smooth had never liked each other. When did they become such good buddies to share secrets, no less have them?

Whatever Bubba saw in Smooth's face assured him it was okay to talk. "She owes money to some guy in Atlantic City. She's got a bad gambling problem."

"Why don't you help her pay it?" he asked before he thought.

"On sheriff's pay? I don't make that kind of money."

Evil, obviously thinking with his stomach, asked, "How does her brother feel about this? What's he going to do?"

"She left all her recipes including the chicken and dressing recipe," Bubba said and gave a sniff. He appeared to be reining in his emotions.

When the guys began arguing over which favorite dish Susan always prepared special for them, Luke left.

Mary's little reprieve was over. He needed to explain he was going nowhere. She needed him as much as he needed her.

As soon as Luke stepped out the door and away from the well-lit parking lot, something didn't feel right. No loitering smokers. No necking lovers. He could hear the thumping of the music behind him and the swooshing of traffic on the interstate nearby. No one hovered in the shadows.

He headed down the crumbling sidewalk, keeping his eyes open for Chet and his cousins. They loved setting up ambushes between the Sandbox and the diner. The pervert and his moron cousins so far hadn't been successful, more due to luck than any special martial arts skills he had developed over the years. But in time they would figure out a way for all three to take him down for sure. Fortunately for some redneck reason, they believed a gun wasn't sporting and preferred to keep it up close and personal.

Once he had the diner in sight, the wind picked up, causing a shiver to shake his body to the bones. Wishing he'd picked up his jacket out of Mary's leased car, he hunched his shoulders and walked a little faster.

He stopped across the street from the diner. Framed in the large glass window, Mary still sat in the same booth.

A sigh whispered between his lips. Relieved to see she was okay and still at the diner, he berated himself for leaving her alone. No matter what Jorge said about giving her forty-eight hours, Luke had a feeling Jorge wasn't long on keeping promises.

She was beautiful, sitting there talking with Susan. He watched as she said something to Susan and then her forehead wrinkled with concern as she listened to her friend.

He must've made a move or caught her attention somehow, as she looked outside and shook her head.

Shake your head all you want, sweetheart, but you and I are going home together tonight. Someone needed to keep an eye on her and he didn't trust just anyone.

"They're looking cozy."

"They're friends," Luke said as he turned to face Evil. The man had stealthy moves.

"I would tell Mary to be careful what she tells her friend." The other man lit a cigarette and tossed the match into the street. "She owes money to Jorge. While she was going to the cooking school in New York, it appears she found out she enjoyed playing Blackjack and other card games in nearby Atlantic City. She was good at first, but she began losing and couldn't stop. You know, always the next hand will be the big one."

"A bit of a strange coincidence, wouldn't you say?" he said sarcastically. He didn't believe in coincidences.

"It's a small world after all." A smile flitted across the dark-haired man's face.

His statement recalled a comment Mary had made about Evil.

"How come you know so much about Susan. For that matter, how did you find out about Mary?"

Evil stood completely still as if he wasn't sure how to answer. Finally, when he moved he took a deep draw off the cigarette as he stared at the ground. Either he was about to lie or wanted to tell only part of the truth.

A trail of smoke fluttered by Luke's face as a car passed, pushing them into the shadows. Before he answered, Evil stared hard across the street, his eyes glittering out into the darkness.

"I have my sources. And I can promise you they're accurate."

Luke didn't want to think his best friend was betraying him, playing some sick game to throw him off. But it wouldn't be the first time a friend screwed him over.

Another car passed by followed by a truck with music blasting out of the cab. Then the street was quiet again.

"You know, you never told me what Mary had over Jorge. I assume the reason I saw Lazaro tonight was that he's tired of being blackmailed." Evil took a last draw and dropped the butt into the gutter.

"It's not like you think." He really wasn't in the mood to explain or mince words with his friend.

"Then explain it to me. I have other friends interested in helping."

That got Luke's attention. The last thing he needed was Evil to bring in his Birmingham contacts into the mix. Fuck. A mob war in Sand City was the last thing he needed. Eighteen months in St. Clair would be chump change compared to getting in the middle of two crime organizations clashing.

"No. I'll handle it."

Actually, he and Mary would handle it. They would find that evidence somehow.

He sensed Evil staring at him as if he wanted to read his mind.

Evil finally turned away. "Okay. Call me if you need me."

Then he loped down the street, staying in the shadows.

Luke couldn't remember feeling so alone. He wanted to talk with his old man, but his dad worried about him enough and didn't need more added to his prayer list.

He turned his attention back to Mary and Susan. Okay, it was time to face the woman he loved. No way would he believe her lame story about not needing him and offering herself to a creep like Lazaro. Like he would let her. Over his dead body.

Problem was, Lazaro probably would be more than happy to make sure the last part happened.

Chapter Thirty-Nine

Mary watched as Luke walked into the diner, his lanky frame stalking across the floor, easing between the tables.

She'd seen he'd returned but remained standing across the street. At that point, there was no way she could go through with it. Pushing him away again would be impossible. When he'd left earlier, she'd never been more afraid in her life, afraid he wouldn't return, afraid she'd made a mistake, afraid to die alone. Overall, she was too selfish, too needy to keep him safe.

"You and I need to talk." His dark eyes were so cold, she wanted to say no, but knew he was right.

"I'll leave you two alone." Susan stood and slipped around Luke without a protest from Mary.

"What do you want to talk about?" Her voice shook a little.

Considering how mad he appeared, she expected he would sit across from her. When he slid in next to her, pushing her to the corner, she knew, though he was still angry, he wasn't about to let her get away with pushing him away again.

"First, we're going to talk about Susan and what she told you," he stated in a cool, no-nonsense voice.

Tamping down the little rebellious girl from long ago that would love to tell him to go to hell, the reasonable grown woman instead said, "She owes Jorge a lot of money."

"And?" Luke ran his hand down her arm. In comfort, she believed. It was working.

"When she saw him in here, she thought he was looking for her. So she made an agreement with her brother to sell her share of the diner. It'll pay off Jorge, but she decided it was best to move away. Bubba's refusing to go with her. I told her it was a lot for him to take in, to give him time. If he really loves her, he'll follow."

Luke hadn't looked one bit surprised by everything she said. She raised her eyebrows. "You knew?"

"I saw Bubba at the Sandbox. He told us the story."

"Us?" She could just imagine the type of women that hung out at a dive like the Sandbox.

"Evil and Smooth were there too."

His thumb grazed her check. His dark eyes gazed into hers. She probably sounded like a jealous shrew.

"I guess we can mark her off our list of suspects. If she had the evidence, she wouldn't be giving everything up here," she said.

"Yeah, who should we suspect at this point? That's something else we need to consider. Jorge and his organization may not be the only ones after the evidence."

"What do you mean?"

"It was something Evil said to me tonight." He began to trace a pattern on her arm. Tingling lines followed his fingers. How could a man absently touching her turn her on so much? "Word must be getting out and we need to speed up our search for the key and the evidence."

"I thought we decided to give up on the key."

"If by some odd chance Lazaro is telling the truth, that means someone else has an agenda. Can you think of anyone that would wish you dead?"

Thinking of dancers she'd unknowingly insulted or may have hurt when she married the eligible bachelor Vincent Hayden, none came to mind that would wait years later to kill her.

"Not a soul." She shook her head.

"That's what I figured. There's a good possibility the person is after me."

"What do you mean?"

"I haven't seen Chet all day. That's unusual. Rarely a day goes by that he doesn't threaten me. I had always thought he would keep it personal and not involve others, but the other day he'd brought his cousins to beat the shit out of me. Luckily, Evil and Smooth were there and helped. Chet must be getting desperate or he believes he has something on me. By the way, his oldest cousin was a demolition expert in the Army."

"That's rather convenient." She tilted her head. "You think Chet broke in and stole the key?"

"At one time I would include Bubba or Susan in the mix. But they're wrapped up in their own affair. I have to say, yeah, I believe Chet is one of our suspects."

"I think you're wrong. Otherwise, he would've done something more drastic to you by now. But let's say that's the case, then we need to include your buddies, Smooth and Evil."

"Smooth and Evil?"

"There's Smooth's new car."

"No crime in owning a new car."

"If you don't have a job to speak of and own a car like that, there's some type of crime going on. And how often has Evil provided information that only a person up to no good would know?" She couldn't help but needle Luke about that. He had to see the light on that point.

"Evil always had a knack for finding out dirt on people. He has connections. I did turn down his offer to bring in some friends from Birmingham. Last thing we need is a mob war. Evil and Smooth have looked out for my back many times. I still say it's a toss-up between Jorge and Chet."

"Well, what do we do now?"

"We take you home and get some rest. It's been a long day and your mom'll be asking for you bright and early in the morning."

So it was going to be like that? He'd pretend she hadn't told him to walk away. As they stood, he reached for her elbow, and out of pure orneriness, as her mom would say, she jerked it away.

"What is it about you and resting?"

"Now, Mary." His voice emerged husky with a thread of command running through it.

He stood and waited next to the booth.

She looked at the hand he held out. The hairs on the back of her neck and arms stood straight up, not in anger, but from how much he turned her on. A little of the old-timey, machismo attitude did it for her especially when she'd already experienced his gentle touch.

How could she protect him when she melted every time he touched her? Or when he got all ape-man in protecting her?

Growing up with a single mom and no dad and only the odd boyfriend of her mom's for a male example, she craved a strong male figure in her life. A man who would stand by her through thick and thin. She always believed that was why she fell in love so fast with her husband. She'd been lucky he'd been good to her too. From what she'd seen in Luke, her luck was holding. Deep inside, he was a good man, just rough around the edges.

She placed her hand in his. She admitted she liked him acting all heroic. She had until she reached home to hatch a plan that would keep Luke safe and out of harm's way while leaving his male ego intact.

<<<>>>

Mary followed Luke's broad shoulders as they stepped into his house to check on his dad before heading to her home.

Reverend Blackwood had company.

Mary wanted to rub her eyes to clear them, for surely she imagined it.

Sue Marie Coleman stood in the middle of the large country kitchen, wearing a black and red apron over her gray and purple dress. The words printed on the apron demanded *Kiss The Cook* and a few splotches of flour and what looked to be apple pie filling covered part of the K across her large bosom.

And it just so happened, the Reverend had a matching splotch on the lower portion of his chest. Exactly twelve inches lower on his body than Sue Marie's. Luke's dad was a good foot taller than Sue Marie.

Mary bit the inside of her mouth to keep from grinning too big or giggling.

"Well, Dad, is Miss Coleman teaching you how to cook finally?" Luke swiped his finger across his dad's chest and sniffed the cinnamon goo before washing it off beneath the running faucet.

"I thought you were keeping an eye on Mary's place tonight." The tall man blushed yet pulled Sue Marie to his side. "We enjoy each other's company," he added in a firm voice Mary recognized. Luke had the same tone when he was serious.

Mary looked at Luke.

How was he handling seeing his dad with another woman? Other than confused, he appeared a little worried. Was he worried his dad's new relationship would overshadow the one he had with his mom?

"I came by to check on you, to make sure you were okay." Luke chuckled. "I guess I should stop worrying about you, huh?"

Zeke looked down with tenderness at Sue Marie. "Yeah, I guess you could say that."

"Mary and I'll leave and let you two get back to your pie," Luke said while his head bobbed up and down. The glint in his eyes told Mary he'd be okay with this new turn of events.

Luke pulled Mary by the hand toward the door when Zeke grabbed Luke's arm.

"I thought about not telling you, but..." He glanced at Mary. "I think it's important for you to know in case it had something to do with protecting Mary."

Mary bumped into Luke as he came to a stop.

"What's wrong, Dad?" Concern washed over Luke's face and filled his voice.

Zeke opened and closed his mouth twice before he appeared to finally gather his thoughts. His struggle with what to say bothered Mary, especially as he was a man known for speaking his mind.

"I ran Chet off Mary's property earlier, caught him peeking in her kitchen window. Not sure what he intended, but he claimed he was looking for her."

"What?" Luke barked.

Thankfully, Zeke didn't let go of his son. Luke's body began to shake. His face reddened and he tugged at the hold, but his father and Mary held on.

"Let go. Both of you," Luke said so softly that it scared her.

She released his hand. Between panic for Luke and sympathy for Chet, well, almost sympathy—the man was an idiot for pushing his guilt onto another—she was unsure of what to do next. Besides, what the heck was he doing at her house?

"Maybe I need to go with you," his dad volunteered.

"Come. Stay. It won't stop me from finishing this. He shouldn't have involved Mary in our quarrel." He looked down at his dad's hand. "Now let me go."

"Son, don't you think it's time to let the past go?"

Luke looked at his dad and then pointedly at Sue Marie. "It appears that you have."

"Thirteen years is a long time to grieve for anyone. Your mom was a good woman that loved us both. She would want us to have a normal life and not tear ourselves up each time we thought of her." Luke's dad released his grip.

Luke narrowed his eyes, shooting a look at Sue Marie and then his dad. With a nod, he stared out the window over the sink.

Was he okay with his dad admitting he was going on with his life finally? Mary stepped back. She was unsure of why she felt the need, but it grabbed Luke's attention.

Pain and sorrow crossed his face, showing how much he struggled with day-to-day living since his mom had died. From what Mary had seen so far, his dad had been totally unprepared to deal with a twelve-year-old boy's misinterpretation of what had happened that day. Every decision made since had been colored for both of them by that one moment in time. Only now his dad was willing to move on and Luke felt too guilty to do the same. Guilt, especially the misplaced type, was a horrible feeling to let go.

Luke continued to stare at Mary as if he wanted her to say something.

"Luke?" She stepped closer and touched his face. Pain flickered across his face.

He lifted her hand to his lips and kissed her fingers. "I'm sorry if I scared you. I never wanted to do that. Dad's right. I have to let go of the past. Funny, that's the same thing you'd told me. It's good to know I have two people who care about me."

And that she did. In fact, she loved him, but now wasn't the time to think about that. "Why don't we go home and I'll show you how much I care?"

The big, bad, crazy ex-con Luke Blackwood blushed.

"I'll take going home with you over beating Chet's ass anytime."

"Well, I guess I'll need to keep you busy then." She looked up into those dark-blue eyes and fluttered her eyelashes in the best Southern belle way she knew.

He laughed and placed his arm on her shoulders. Mary noticed how Zeke's and Sue Marie's shoulders relaxed on hearing the sweet sound. The man certainly needed to laugh more often and she wanted to ensure he did.

If only they knew what part Chet played in all of what happened.

Chapter Forty

Nothing outside the dark house looked suspicious as they drove up but Luke felt uneasy with the thought of Chet snooping around. Dry fall leaves hit the windshield as the wind kicked up. A storm coming off the gulf played with the top of the trees surrounding the house, bending and rattling the thin branches.

Luke pulled Mary's car into her garage and shut off the engine. He glanced her way as he opened the driver's door. "Stay here and let me check the house."

"Do you think Chet could still be here?" A small tremble betrayed her fright.

He shrugged his shoulders and pulled her in tight for a second. "There's no way to tell for sure. Though I promise I'll make sure he doesn't nose around again."

"Then I'm coming in too. No matter what you told your dad, you might have a bit of difficulty in stopping your old habit of kicking his butt."

He chuckled. "You're good for me, you know?" Leaning across the front seat he kissed her. Tasting what she'd offered earlier, he wished Chet would jump off a high bridge.

After pulling away, he brushed hair out of her face. "If you insist on coming with me, stay close."

As soon as he walked into the house he felt it even before he found the alarm turned off. Someone had been there or was still hiding inside.

"Did you forget to set the alarm this morning?" he asked in a low voice.

"No. I set the new code before we left."

"Do you still have your gun with you?" Why hadn't he thought to pick up a gun from his dad's?

"Yes. I thought it best to have it with me when I met with Jorge," Mary whispered back.

"Hand it to me." He held his hand out. "Please."

Without hesitation she pulled the small pistol from her purse and placed the handle in his palm. By feeling around the trigger, he flipped off the safety.

"It jerks to the right slightly," she warned in a low voice.

He hoped he wouldn't need it. Too much could go wrong in the dark. He quickly decided the best course was to turn on the lights and hope no one else shot first.

"Stay behind me and close as you can." Her soft, warm body almost distracted him from what he was doing. He took a deep breath and palmed the multi-switches that controlled the outside floodlights and the lights in the living and dining rooms.

No gun shots, no running feet. They were alone in the house from what he could tell so far. Keeping her close by his side, they eased into the kitchen as he hit the light switch.

Mary gasped as Luke cursed the cold-hearted person that had done it. The small teddy bear stretched out in the middle of the kitchen table with a knife through its heart. Someone's sick warning.

How had someone gotten inside? That was when he noticed the backdoor's broken lock in pieces on the floor. Had Chet decided to pay Mary a visit and try to scare her? But how had he turned off the alarm? Using a knife especially on a toy wasn't Chet's style.

"Chet has no imagination to use an impaled stuffed bear as a threat. You're certain you turned on the alarm?" His gaze searched every corner.

"Yes."

She sounded as baffled as he was by the easy way people entered her house.

He watched as she reached for the steak knife.

"We should call Bubba and let him check it for fingerprints."

With a nod of her head, she tossed a towel over the knife and animal. The sight was apparently too much for her despite it being only a stuffed bear.

"Jorge wouldn't be so stupid as to leave prints, but maybe someone else did," she said with her eyes closed.

Something about the teddy bear nagged at Luke.

"Why would Jorge stab a stuffed animal?" he asked, not expecting an answer. "He appears to me a person who would shoot it or tear it apart. Kind of how he did the storage unit or your house the other day. And how would he know what role it played in finding the evidence?"

"So you don't think it was Jorge." Eyes opened wide now, she appeared more frightened by the uncertainty. "So not Jorge or Chet? Then who? Evil? Smooth? We're running out of people we know who are capable of breaking in."

"Or it could be someone Jorge hired, someone who's

hanging around town and hearing the rumors flying. Only thing about that is, someone new is always noticed and I haven't heard of any strangers." He placed the gun on the table and pulled her into his arms. Every time he touched her, he was amazed by how soft she was beneath his callused fingers.

"Call Bubba. Except for the knife and the broken door, I don't think they'd find much, the same as when someone ransacked the place."

"Okay. First, I'll shove the table and chairs against the back door. If anyone tries to get in that way, they'll make a racket."

In moments, Luke with Mary's help barred the back-door the best they could. He then leaned against the counter and pressed the speed dial for Bubba's personal phone number. Being in trouble all the time, he found having Bubba's number came in handy. As soon as the sheriff answered he punched in speaker mode and told him the news.

A few seconds passed without a word from Bubba; he was probably trying to figure out the logistics. What with only a handful of deputies, and from the sound of people shouting in the background, he was not in the office and something had happened.

"I'll be there first thing in the morning or one of my deputies. Don't touch anything. Lock up the place or go somewhere else to stay, but most likely Chet or whoever won't be back tonight. I'll keep an eye out for him and notify my deputies. By the way, we believe we found where the explosives came from. The local mining company had some missing and just notified us. They have a lot to explain." At that moment, another shout came across. It sounded like Susan. "Once we handle that," Bubba continued, "and if the storm doesn't do any damage, one of us will be right over. It'll take a while and we're already spread thin."

"We should be good. We're staying put. I'll protect Mary. See you then."

"Good. We'll call when we're on our way." Then the line went dead.

He turned toward Mary sitting at the table. Her eyelids drooped with her head resting on her arms.

"You heard Bubba. It's late. We need our sleep. Let's set the alarm, for whatever good it will do, and hope the storm blows over fast."

A loud thundering sounded off in the distance. The storm was coming closer and the high wind threats they'd heard on the radio earlier were headed their way.

She lifted her head, blinking as if to clear her vision, and then stood.

"We should be fine until morning. Who knows, Bubba might have an idea by then." She came up to Luke and squeezed him around his waist. "I can't think straight."

"Come on. Take a long, hot bath while I fix us some sandwiches." He squeezed her in return.

Needing more, he covered her mouth with his. He explored the heated warmth with his tongue as she met him with thrusts of her own. The kiss was what they needed. Something better to think of besides the craziness around them. His body told him he wanted more. Hard and aching, he rubbed against her and she groaned long in his mouth. Damn, she was so sweet.

He pulled back and gave her a gentle shove toward the stairs. "Go. Take a bath. I'll have your sandwich ready when you get back."

"Bologna and cheese?"

He chuckled. "Yeah. Cheese melted?"

"Yes, please."

As he listened, water started running about the time the rain let loose and began beating on the tin roof. The sound always brought memories of his childhood and the safe feeling he got from knowing he was inside and warm while it poured outside. His mom always had board games ready. She'd loved games.

Shaking off the sad thoughts, he began pulling together the ingredients for the sandwiches. He noticed in the refrigerator a pitcher of tea and a large jar of dill pickles that would be perfect to go with the meal.

He fought the image of Mary soaking in the tub, her soft skin glistening with beads of water and whatever the stuff women loved to put in their bathwater. One long leg lifting out of the water and her soapy hand gliding up her thigh to the spot he loved to lick.

Damn. He had to stop. Standing in the middle of her kitchen horny and hard was not the right way to greet a woman who had been through enough. Considering Mary's reaction to his advances, chances were she would appreciate it.

He chuckled and shook his head.

Thunder rolled nearer, shaking the house on its foundation. He whipped around to face the backdoor. Someone was banging on the screen. Hell, between the stormy night and the drama going down earlier, he expected to see plenty of gray hair in the mirror tomorrow morning.

He looked at the kitchen door's window and spotted Chet, soaking wet and shivering. Why was the lunatic turning up at Mary's house again and on a night like this? Had he hoped to catch Mary by herself? The sorry sack of scum was going to die.

Luke jerked opened the door and screen and pulled

Chet in by his shirt, lifting him until they could see eye-to-eye.

"What the hell are you doing knocking on Mary's door so late at night? And you better make it a good reason."

Drops of cold water dripped off of Chet's nose and streamed from his hair.

"I came to warn you that Jorge Lazaro plans to kill you and Mary tonight." He squeaked when Luke pushed him against the wall.

"Are you here to help?" Luke kept his fists tight on the shaking man's shirt.

"I...I...couldn't go through with it."

"Why don't I believe you? Maybe we need to call Bubba out here and let him know what you've been up to with a known criminal."

"Bubba ain't sheriff anymore."

The grin that spread across Chet's face made Luke want to smash his fist into it, repeatedly.

"What do you mean? I just spoke to him fifteen minutes ago."

"That was about the same time he turned in his resignation to the mayor. His girl has split town and now he's following her."

Just like Bubba, leaving when he was needed the most.

"How do you know Lazaro?" Luke asked, his tone making clear he wanted the truth.

"He had his guards ask around about you and Mary. I guess someone told him about the times I beat your ass."

"So someone lied. I would imagine it was one of your cousins."

"Yeah. Just wait until I'm voted in as sheriff. You'll be the one sitting in jail to cool off. Only I won't let you out. You can rot in there as far as I care!"

Luke shook the idiot. "How were you to help Lazaro?"

"Dynamite. We use it to take care of tree trunks in the fields. I was to place them under the house."

"And you want me to believe you worried about me?"

"Fuck, no. Mary…I didn't want to blow up a fine piece of—argh!"

One good jab did it. Chet was out cold as he slid down the wall and slumped to the side.

Anxious that Chet's cousins might be nearby, waiting for their leader, Luke checked the windows for strange cars or trucks parked in the shadows. Nothing out there that didn't belong.

He shrugged his shoulders and decided there was no help for it. In the morning, he'd find out who was the interim sheriff. With Bubba gone, he was on his own and needed to make sure Chet gave him no more problems.

Chapter Forty-One

ary checked the belt on her robe again, making sure the tie was tight and all her girly bits were covered. Maybe she was being silly, considering Luke had seen everything, but that was while they were in the moment, making love.

When she walked into the kitchen, she found Luke kneeling on the floor, wiping at muddy tracks with a wad of paper towels. The jacket he wore dripped water.

"What happened?"

"Sorry. I never got around to making your sandwich." He looked up and his gaze followed hers to his hands. "Yeah, that. I had to take care of a few things in your shed and check on the Misfits. It's amazing the varmints that come out of the rain during nights like this." He swiped at the last of the dirt and stood, tossing the soiled sheets into the garbage can.

"No problem. Why don't I put together the sandwiches? Grilled cheese with bologna sounds good." She spotted the sandwich makings sitting on the counter. His animals had drawn his attention before he'd finished. She opened the loaf of bread and pulled out several slices.

When he continued to be quiet, she looked over her shoulder at him.

The twinkle in his dark eyes told her he was thinking of anything but food.

He grinned and said, "I need to take a shower, but I wonder if you could do me a favor." With each word he came closer until she could smell the clean scent of rain-soaked hair. "I would like you to come with me."

"But I've already taken a bath." She was tempted to take him up on his offer.

"Yeah, I know but we can play." A fleeting emotion passed over his face. He was hiding something and she didn't like it at all.

"No. I think I better fix us something to eat before we become too weak."

He grunted.

"Okay." He grinned and came up behind her, clasping her hips, and pulled her against the hardness he was sporting. He whispered near her temple, "It would be best if one of us keeps an ear out for trouble, like tornados. You know the infamous words on every newscast, *it sounded like a freight train.*" He deepened his drawl on the last few words, bringing a bark of laughter from her.

He fooled no one but himself—those marks were not his, his boots were wet and not muddy—but she decided to play along. Eventually he would tell her or she would find out on her own.

<<<>>>

Later, as she stretched out on the bed with the sodas, sandwiches, and chips waiting on the nightstand, she listened to the water running in the shower. The storm started up again, worse than it had earlier. The house shook with each thunder clap.

She'd never been afraid of storms, even in the South with the possibility of tornados. Another thunder clap vibrated through the room. In fact, the sound shot energy through her body, giving an electrified feeling to her skin, turning her on as much as the dirty anticipation of a freshly washed Luke. Realizing the oxymoron twist on her thoughts, she was smiling big when he walked out of the bathroom.

He stopped and stared. The towel he wore around his waist began to show a noticeable bulge.

"Nothing beats finding a near-naked, smiling woman waiting for you on a bed." His eyes blazed with appreciation.

Wearing only a dressing gown and revealing certain parts of her anatomy was one of the lessons she'd learned in Vegas. A woman could inflame a man's lust with a lot of skin, but to reveal only a partial nipple and a little inner thigh drove them wild.

He took a few steps nearer and then dropped his towel.

She leaned forward and gently led him by his sensitive length to her mouth. Opening her mouth, she enjoyed the heat and the feel of satin-covered steel as she ran her tongue around the tip and along his shaft. His gasp was only part of the reward she wanted.

"Oh, Honey. You treat me so good. I don't deserve you."

One broad hand cupped the back of her head as she showed him how much she enjoyed what he had to offer.

Bad boys were so sexy and she believed she'd found one that would be good for her.

She released him and scooted toward the headboard, crooking her finger for Luke to follow. He crawled over the length of the queen-size bed, a lean tiger ready to mount his mate.

He eased the dressing gown off her shoulders and dipped to one taut nipple. Streaks of electricity shot from his mouth over her torso to her groin. The intense pleasure bowed her body, triggering her to beg for more.

He sucked, and then clamping gently around her nipple, he stretched the tip as one hand cupped her other breast, pinching and rolling the tight bead. Before she could catch her breath, he slid his free hand between her thighs and thrust two fingers into her wet heat, inciting a moan of approval from her. She met the sensation with a craving for something bigger.

Unable to resist her own exploring, she rubbed her hands up his broad shoulders, delighting in the swells and hard muscles moving beneath her fingers. He moved back from her and nudged her legs apart, making room for his hips.

Lightning lit up the room as she looked into his eyes, lust and emotion shining from their dark depths. She had no doubt the man loved her. Never had she believed she could fall in love with another bad boy. At least when he appeared the bad boy to the world, he showed his true self to her. He was a good man trying to forget a horrible past and forgive himself for an event that was beyond his control.

She grabbed the sides of his head and pulled him down for a kiss. Lips, tongues, and even teeth came into play as he thrust inside her, filling her, stretching her until she wasn't sure she could take anymore but begged for more. Her body quaked as she came and he quickly followed while at the same time, thunder shook the house.

When he finally rolled to the side, kissing her one more time, he pulled her into his arms. Her head rested on his shoulder. Their heavy breathing and the drumming of rain on the tin roof broke the silence. The storm was finally dissipating.

Tonight was more than just making love. They'd come to a new crossroads. Tomorrow they would decide what they wanted from each other. Either a commitment, or a decision that only extreme circumstances had brought them together and they weren't meant to be.

She could see the three of them living together on her farm. Then it would be his farm too. Her mom already liked Luke and from how much satisfaction Luke received while working on the farm house, he would surely be happy to stay.

She lightly dragged her nails across his chest and watched his small male nipple tighten in response. His hand covered hers, stopping her play.

"I'll be happy to oblige you in a few more minutes, Babe."

"Okay. I'll wait but only for a little while." She pressed her nose into his chest hair, inhaling his clean, masculine scent.

The chuckle he released brought a smile to her face. He laughed so much more now. His desire to track down and pulverize Chet had obviously been placed to the side.

"See. Isn't this much better than finding Chet and beating him to a bloody pulp?"

His body tensed beside her.

Why had she mentioned that man's name? Stupid. Open mouth, insert foot during a sexy time. She snuggled closer and was happy to feel his muscles relax while an important part of his anatomy came to attention.

By the time they fell back on the bed, panting from their lovemaking, she had another smile on her face and hoped he did also. The room was too dark to tell for sure. The last twenty-four hours had been rough, to say the least, so once she snuggled against Luke she drifted to sleep.

In her dreams, a strange pressure over her nose, mouth, and arms wouldn't go away no matter how she tossed her head or reached for the covers. Pitch-black darkness met her eyes when she finally thought to force them open. Was she still dreaming?

She whimpered when a sting followed by a burning sensation shot into her thigh. Seconds later, she felt the sheet wrap tight around her from mouth to ankles and someone lifted her from the bed, and whatever covered her eyes fell away. Through her fuzzy vision, she barely made out Luke struggling with what looked like two shadows.

When she awoke from the murkiness of her dreams, she was sitting up and unable to move. Then there was a pounding in her head and an odd taste in her mouth. As her eyes slowly focused, it was to a new nightmare. The pounding was Chet slamming his fist into Luke's stomach as two men dressed in black with ski masks held him between them. Jorge stood to the side with his two bodyguards watching Luke's naked body bow with each punch.

"Stop! Leave him alone!"

The men continued their horrible beating.

Hadn't she screamed those words?

They would kill him and she refused to let another person she loved be killed by Jorge's command.

"If they don't stop and he dies," she glared at Jorge, "I'll never tell you where the evidence is."

That got his attention. He raised his hand. "Enough, Chet. We mustn't upset the lady."

Chet hit Luke one last time. "He deserves a lot worse. The SOB tied me up and threw me into the tool shed. I was stuck there for hours until my cousins found me." He swiped sweat off his forehead with a sleeve. His beady eyes turned toward her. Tied to the chair with only a sheet covering her bare body, she was helpless. "Give me ten minutes with the woman and she'll tell you anything you want to know when I'm through." The leer he gave caused her stomach to work toward her throat.

"Over my dead body," Luke said barely above a whisper.

"That can be arranged," Chet goaded.

"It won't be necessary." Jorge waved the black-clothed men to shove Luke into a chair. "Tie him up. We can't have him trying any heroics. Isn't that right, Brandon?"

Brandon "Smooth" Rogan stepped out of the shadows. "Yeah. Wouldn't it be a shame if we had to break an arm or leg?"

"Smooth, what kind of trick is this?" Chet began backing away from the man.

Not that Luke's friend made a move to help, but more for the reason Smooth wore a bulletproof vest with the letters FBI blazoned across the front. If the uniform wasn't enough to make a criminal rethink, the gun in Smooth's hand insured everyone stayed back.

"Where's your brother?" Luke asked.

"Chasing his tail." Smooth grinned, his eyes deadly cold.

Chet pulled a gun from the back of his jeans and aimed

it at Smooth. "We outnumber you." He nodded toward Jorge. "We can hide his body out at my farm."

"Idiot. He's with me." Jorge pushed the muzzle of Chet's gun toward the floor. "Took you long enough to get here," he said to Smooth.

That explained the nice car. Though she wasn't sure who helped pay for it, the government or Jorge. Her money was on Jorge.

"I had to cover my tracks and make sure my brother didn't follow." Smooth walked over to Mary and lifted a lock of her hair, rubbing it between his fingers. "I see you have everything under control here."

She glared, wishing she could move out of his reach.

"You said you'd take care of him." Jorge frowned, not pleased by Smooth's answer. "We can't have him prying."

"I've been careful. He has no idea." Smooth released her hair and moved in front of Luke. "Did you know that big brother's FBI too? He'd been investigating a case in Marystown when he was ordered to check on your little darling over here."

"I've always been told to watch out for the quiet ones." Luke struggled with the ropes holding his hands and feet to the chair.

"Yeah, but who's tied up and naked as the day he was born?" Smooth eyed one of Chet's cousins loitering a bit closer to Luke. "Chet, tell the meathead to step away."

Chet lifted his chin and pointed to a space to the side. The black-clad hulk moved.

"It's a shame you're not as easy to kill as her husband," Smooth said to Luke as if he was talking about the time of day.

She gasped, looking at Jorge and back at Smooth. All this time she'd been blaming the wrong person. Then the truth clicked in her head...he was the FBI agent who met with Vincent that fateful day her husband's car exploded. The smug look he gave warned he was aware she understood his connection.

"You blew up my car," she said between gritted teeth. Her face heated and she shook with anger. "Jorge, did he blow up mine and Vincent's cars per your instructions?"

"Now, Honey, it appears he was a little over-enthusiastic about his job. We had a talk and he won't be doing it again without talking with me first." Jorge shook his head.

"Oh, that makes me feel a whole lot better," she muttered.

"You know this situation all started because of you," Jorge said.

He dared to blame all this on her?

"Don't let him get to you," Luke warned.

"Please enlighten me." She'd better get a hold of her temper or she could kiss hers and Luke's butts goodbye.

"You kept nagging Vincent to turn over state's evidence. To go straight and get a regular job." Jorge moved in front of her and glowered. "My best friend and the best enforcer a guy could have and you pussy-whipped him into turning his back on me. That I can never forgive."

How could she argue with him? He was right. How many times had she wished she'd kept her mouth shut? She'd still have Vincent. She glanced over to Luke. But was she willing to miss out in knowing such a man? She was torn between her loyalties, one for a dead man who planned to change and the other very much alive, at least for now, who worked so hard to prove he was good enough for her. He probably now understood she was the one who needed to prove good enough for him.

"From what Mary told me about Vinny, he wouldn't do

something he didn't want to do. So was it really her fault."
Luke started laughing. "Boo-hoo, your friend loved a woman
more than you," Luke derided.

Jorge raised his arm to backhand Luke but stopped
when Smooth stepped between them.

"Our energies would be best spent finding the evidence
you're so worried about." Smooth pointed the gun at Mary.
"If you had told me she had something on you, I would've
taken care of her in the beginning before I let her move to
Alabama."

"What do you mean *let* me move?" Horrors of how she
was manipulated shook her.

Smooth's laugh sent shivers down her spine, followed by
a queasiness sweeping through her body. She'd never heard
such a vile laugh and tried to lean away as the FBI agent
moved closer.

"Do you really think it was by chance that you found
this farmhouse? It was easy to send info to all the major real
estate offices in Las Vegas. They did the rest of the work."
He glanced at the clock above her head over the mantel.
"Enough talk about how we got here, time for you to tell us
where the information is."

Nausea pulled at Mary's throat. She'd been so close to
death since she arrived and was unaware of it. All the time
she'd thought she'd left that life behind, she'd been fooling
no one but herself. Maybe it was time to tell Jorge the truth.
She had no idea where the key or evidence was. It would
sign her death certificate but she could no longer fight the
obvious conclusion.

"Who is in control of this situation?" Jorge's ego was
showing, apparently he detested how Smooth was taking
over.

While the two men argued, the strangest thing

happened. One of Chet's cousins slipped behind her and began to loosen the cord around her wrists. What kind of trick was this?

Just as her hands were freed, the man's movements behind Mary had caught Smooth's attention. "Hey! What the fuck is your problem? Keep your distance from her."

The cousin stepped to the side, pulling their attention away.

When Smooth pointed his gun at the black-clad man, Chet punched his cousin in the shoulder. "Stupid! Don't make a man nervous when he's holding a gun, and take off that stupid mask." He grabbed and jerked it off his cousin. "What the..."

All eyes turned toward Evil. Why had he been pretending to be Chet's cousin?

"Hi, Chet. Brother." He nodded at Jorge and his guards.

The tension in the room rose to the level of a nuclear disaster. He'd untied her hands, but was it to rush her demise or to help? Sure, he was FBI, but so was his brother who was obviously the mastermind over the insane charade.

"What is your brother doing here?" Jorge pointed his men toward Evil.

As they reached for him, Evil lifted his hand, palm out. "Whoa, boys. I have something you've been looking for." He placed two fingers into the front pocket of his jeans and pulled out a chain with a key dangling from the end.

The same key that had hung on the teddy bear.

Chapter Forty-Two

L uke remained still. At least it explained why the *cousin* had untied his hands earlier before Smooth had complained. But was Evil waiting for him to make a move? To kill him or help him? He had no idea they were FBI. So who could say if one was a traitor or both?

The only one he was certain about was Jorge. He obviously wanted to keep him alive until he got his answers from Mary.

A glance over at Mary assured him she was okay. She shrugged, just as confused by the turn of events as he was.

Then he remembered seeing Evil, still dressed as Chet's cousin, standing behind Mary for a little while. Had he untied her too? If he had, that would mean he was helping. Right? Everything would become clear soon.

He looked down and shook his head. Hell, he was naked. How could he help if that was Evil's intention? Though he could fight with the best of them bare knuckles, he doubted he would win against men holding guns. That only happened in the movies.

"Brandon, is that the key you told me about?" Before he could answer, Jorge turned back to Evil. "Give it to me."

Jorge lunged for the key and Evil grabbed the man's gun at the same time, jerking his arm up and pulling. A crack of bone vibrated through the room. Jorge landed at Evil's feet, holding his arm and groaning. Evil quickly aimed the gun at the boss before the bodyguards could pull out theirs.

Well, maybe not just in the movies. Luke couldn't believe how Evil moved like some type of fighting machine.

"Okay, fellows, drop your guns on the floor or I'll make your boss suffer a little more."

When his guards hesitated, Evil stepped on Jorge's arm. He screamed like a girl.

"Do what he says or you're fired!" Jorge glared at his men until they pulled the guns from beneath their jackets and slid them across the floor to Evil.

Evil kicked one to Luke while keeping an eye on Smooth. "Here. Cover me."

The man's brother had the strangest smirk on his face. Was he changing sides? Smooth could easily shoot his older brother.

When Luke leaned down to pick up the gun, Chet muttered, "Stupid lousy agent." The man lifted a foot to take a step toward Evil.

"You better not move," Luke said as he aimed the gun at his old nemesis. Chet's usual red face paled and he didn't even place his foot back on the floor.

Out of the corner of Luke's eye, he watched as Evil turned the gun on his brother.

"Okay, brother, time for you to hand over your weapon."

Smooth cocked his head and grinned wider. "You really think I'll hand it over, big brother?"

"I wish you would. I'll hate to be known as the man who

killed his own brother." Evil looked almost relaxed, like he'd rehearsed this interplay before.

"I should've killed you while you fought with Lazaro." Smooth appeared as calm as his brother. The man had ice running through his veins. "Telling you how rich we could be won't change your mind, will it?" Evil shook his head. "There's so much money out there waiting for someone to come and grab it. I refuse to go to bed hungry again."

"This isn't the way to go about it," Luke said, wanting to bring this crazy drama to an end and take Mary somewhere safe.

As if she knew he was worried about her, Mary grabbed one of the guard's guns and pointed it at the Vegas boss, providing Luke with the opportunity to help Evil. The woman was amazing. She showed a calmness most experienced people couldn't achieve during a dangerous situation like this.

Smooth looked at Luke, keeping a gun on his brother. His smile had disappeared.

"What do you know about going to bed hungry or having your dad beat you until you pee blood? Oh, yeah, you mope around town acting like you're the only kid to grow up without a ma. Well, at least you didn't watch your dad bury your own mother in a field." Smooth began to shake.

"What are you talking about?" Evil took a step toward his brother.

"You really believed that load of crock that dad told you about the carny? You were always such a pussy." Tears streamed down Smooth's face while his hands shook in anger.

Luke wasn't sure what made him do it, but he swung his gun and fired at the same time Smooth and Evil shot at each other. Then all hell broke loose. The lights went out. Shouting filled the room. Smoke disoriented Luke as men in helmets, with guns drawn, burst through the front door and flowed into the living room.

"FBI! Everyone hit the floor! Put your weapons down!"

Luke stretched out face first on the floor, pushing the gun off to the side while the agents surrounded everyone. A knee jabbed into the small of his back and held him in place while rough hands handcuffed him.

"Stay here!" a deep, unfamiliar voice instructed.

Yeah, right. Not like he had a lot of options, what with being naked and all.

He heard Mary telling one of the agents what had happened, all in an even tone. How many women could go through what she did and still look so beautiful and keep it together so well?

He looked over to where they worked on Evil. When he heard his friend cough, he released his held breath. It was good to know he was still alive.

Chet and the one cousin along with Jorge's men were led out, handcuffed and looking downcast.

Then he checked on Smooth's condition. The EMT kneeling over him held defibrillator paddles over the wounded man's chest and nodded at his co-worker. Twice he applied the paddles before shaking his head.

A girlish scream came from Jorge when an agent pulled his arms behind his back and locked on the handcuffs. Luke felt no shame chuckling over the man's pain. He deserved that and so much more for terrorizing Mary.

He heard a shout outside. Someone had found Chet's other cousin knocked out and tied to a tree in a thicket nearby.

Hands grabbed Luke's upper arms and jerked him to his

feet. The agent had a mean glint to his eyes. Obviously, he wanted to be anywhere but where he was.

"What are you, Braveheart?" he asked smirking.

"They caught me at a bad time," Luke simply said.

"Yeah, I bet they did," the agent said as he leered at Mary wrapped in a sheet.

"You keep your eyes on me, asshole." No way would he allow anyone to mistreat or think ill of Mary.

"You better watch that mouth, boy." The agent jerked him by the handcuffs toward the front door.

"Hey, Schmidt, bring him over here. I need to talk with the fellow." An older agent dressed in a tie and jacket, unlike the others who had rushed in earlier, motioned for the agent to have Luke sit on the couch.

Apparently Schmidt wasn't too happy with the change of directions and made sure Luke had a few bruises from *clumsily walking* into furniture on the way to the couch.

"J.T. tells me that you had no connections to Lazaro and his shenanigans, except for protecting this little lady." The agent and Luke glanced at Mary. She adjusted the sheet higher over her chest in self-consciousness. "In fact, that you might even have saved his life. Is that correct, Mr. Blackwood?" The agent folded his arms across his barrel chest and looked down his nose at Luke.

He wanted to tell the agent to stick it where the sun didn't shine, until he glanced over to Evil. They'd moved his friend to a gurney and he was listening to the conversation. Something about the worried look on Evil's face and the pleading in Mary's eyes warned him his answer could have long-lasting consequences.

"J.T., huh?" Luke asked, looking again at Evil. The wounded man nodded and gave a grimace as they pushed the gurney out of the room. Upon seeing another agent had stopped to talk with Mary, Luke returned his attention to the man he guessed was J.T.'s boss. "I did what was necessary to protect the woman I love and my best friend."

The big guy dropped his arms to the side and smiled, showing a small space between the two upper front teeth. For some reason, seeing something so human and unexpected calmed Luke.

"Let's see if we can get you out of those handcuffs and into some pants. Unless you enjoy sitting there hanging in the breeze?"

Luke ignored the man's laughter and shook his head. "No. So if you'll let me take Mary upstairs, we can get decent enough for more questions."

"Sure." The agent nodded and then looked at Schmidt. "Release him and throw him the blanket off the couch. No need to let him show off any more than necessary." The man began laughing again.

"I'm glad to be so entertaining." Luke shot Schmidt a hard look when the agent unlocked the handcuffs none too gently.

Luke took Mary's arm and led her to the stairs, making sure to keep Smooth's body out of sight. How would the FBI write up his killing one of their own? He had no doubt his bullet was the one that took out Evil's brother. Smooth had been corrupt but would that matter to the government?

He would hate to leave Mary behind and go back to prison. If not for the murder, for being in possession of a firearm and firing it.

Was that why Evil and his boss appeared to insist he claimed to save them? Well, he'd be damned. He'd never believed to be thankful to any branch of law enforcement.

As soon as they reached the top of the stairs, he dropped

the blanket and scooped up Mary. He carried her down the hallway to her room.

Once they reached her closet, his brow wrinkled as he studied her. Except for a couple of bruises, she appeared to be fine. In fact, too fine to allow those bozos to be near her. He'd keep an eye on her during their questioning, making sure they treated her with proper respect.

"I'm fucking tired of those men leering at you. Let's get dressed," he said as he slowly released her. The sheet fell at her feet. She eased down his body, her bare breasts firm against his torso.

"You read my mind." She gave him a trembling grin.

Despite the full house, he pressed her full length against his body and kissed her, hard, giving her an example of what would come later.

He decided, once he pulled on some clothes, he would be the one asking the FBI questions.

Chapter Forty-Three

Mary kept her gaze from drifting to Luke as they pulled on their clothes. She hoped her face didn't show how worried she was about his silence. For the last ten minutes he hadn't touched her or said a word. She understood they needed to hurry back downstairs, yet she still felt nervous about what the FBI planned to do. With Luke being an ex-convict, he could be in a lot of trouble. For now, she would take one problem at a time. Especially those she believed the FBI would bring up first.

"Are you worried about what the FBI will do when I tell them we don't have the evidence? Do you think they'll suspect us of lying, playing some game?" She stood in front of the mirror to make sure every button was fastened, only glancing over to Luke when he didn't respond.

He looked as if he'd lost his best friend. She guessed in a way he had. From what she could tell he'd been closer to Evil than Smooth, and he'd found out in the worst sort of way his best friend had hidden an important part of his life.

"I hadn't really thought about it. Then again, we haven't

promised them anything." He shrugged as he tucked in his shirt. He'd left some clothes the other day, in case he needed to change out of paint-stained ones. At least, that was what he'd claimed. She recalled how excited she'd been when she came across his shirt and pants hanging in her closet. "Come on. We better get moving before they come looking for us. We might as well get it over with."

She guessed he was right. Only she had a good reason to think the window looked like a great way to escape. The tree was near enough. And sticking around didn't sound appealing to her. She never had much luck when it came to the FBI.

"I'll be by your side all the way," he said.

Warmth heated her chilled skin. With only a few words from the man who had protected her during a horrendous time, she felt safer than ever. But she needed to stand on her own two feet. They could be back to boss and handyman tomorrow. Not one word of love had left his lips. He enjoyed the sex, but what about a commitment?

"You don't have to," she said softly. She hated feeling so needy, wanting to hear the three words from him she craved to say back

A knot formed in her chest with the thought of Luke not wanting to be around her any more. She'd been nothing but trouble.

When Luke had stood up to Jorge and Smooth, she knew he was the type of man she wanted to be with for the rest of her life. She'd realized falling in love with him might not be enough. But would he want to stay with a woman who brought trouble to his family and friends? Because of her, he nearly got killed.

"Now's not the time to argue. Let's get downstairs." He waved her toward the bedroom door.

She hesitated, wanting his arms around her, holding her. No. No. Time to depend on herself again.

"Is something wrong?" His brow furrowed in concern.

Why did he have to be so nice to her? Tears welled up and she rapidly blinked. She refused to let him see her cry again. She hated crying. What a silly emotion to have at a time like this. Why hadn't she cried while Jorge and Smooth held a gun on her? They might've shown her some compassion.

No. She was never that type. Even when a police officer pulled her over for speeding, she couldn't force a single tear out to get out of the ticket.

Embarrassed, the tears began to stream down her face. She loved this man and he would leave her soon. Hadn't her father and her husband left her behind? So why wouldn't Luke want a different life, one without dread of the past coming back again? How could she live there, knowing she would see him every day, and not touch him?

"Oh, Baby, please stop crying. I promise everything will be okay. The FBI doesn't have a reason to arrest you." Then he did what she'd truly wanted so badly, he pulled her into his arms.

She sighed. A feeling of safety flowed through her.

"I'm sorry. It's not the FBI. I want to tell you—"

"You two better be on the way down those steps in two seconds!" The agent below sounded impatient.

Luke wiped her tears away and kissed each eyelid. "Come on. It'll be okay. I promise." He kept an arm around her as they made their way down.

That strong arm meant so much to her. Security, affection, maybe she wouldn't be alone.

<<<>>>

"I haven't introduced myself. I'm Special Agent in Charge Roy Reese." He held out his hand.

When it looked as if Luke would refuse to take it, she nudged him with her elbow. Why antagonize the FBI?

The agent kept his hand out until Luke shook it.

"You don't need to worry about shooting the younger Rogan. J.T. confirmed you saved him and Ms. Hayden. We're not sure which firearm caused the fatal wound. Still, you'll just need to answer a few more questions."

"What can we help you with?" Mary tried to keep her tone even and nonchalant, but did a horrible job as her voice squeaked at the end.

Luke gently squeezed her arm, reminding her of his presence.

Special Agent Reese's gapped-tooth grin and sparklingly dark eyes encouraged her to trust him. She felt comfortable enough to smile back. He appeared to be one of the real good guys.

"We've been watching Lazaro for some time. Our sources say you have some evidence of money laundering with a spattering of sports bribery, and maybe a couple disappearances thrown in." Then his face became blank as he looked away from her. "I'm really sorry what happened to your husband. He was doing the right thing when he got killed."

"Vincent wasn't a good person, but he'd been a good husband. I tell myself his death was destined to be, but I can't help but wonder if I hadn't tried to change him, would he still be alive?"

"Ma'am, I learned men like him rarely live to a ripe old age, and few people can make them change if they don't want to."

"That's what I tell myself." She hugged Luke's arm. His heat soaking into her side reminded her she had a new love and he was a good man, no matter his past. "I guess you want to know what little I know about the evidence."

Leaving out the part about digging up Vincent's grave, she told the special agent about the box with the key hanging around the teddy bear's neck. And how the key had been stolen and where they had looked for whatever the key would fit and then about the evidence in the picture frame.

"Is this the key you were talking about?" The agent held up the key Evil had dropped during the fight.

"I believe so. It looks like it." Since Evil had the key, she figured the FBI had also tried to find what it fit. "So you didn't have any luck either?"

Special Agent Reese shook his head. "And the picture and frame, are they still here?"

"Yeah. I believe so." She looked at Luke. He walked over to the closet and pulled out the picture of Audrey Hepburn from the closet.

A hum of appreciation came from the big man. "I liked her. Especially in that great, old black-and-white thriller, *Wait Until Dark.*"

She could see why some men were turned on by Audrey Hepburn's fragile beauty. Mary stepped closer to Luke. Thankfully, he appeared to enjoy a woman with a fuller figure.

"That was Vinny's favorite movie too. I'll never forget the first time he asked me to watch it with him. You know, the part where she believes the bad guy is dead and he grabs her out of the dark..." She waited until he nodded. "I jumped so high, I got a cramp in my leg."

Vinny had teased her for weeks afterwards. She smiled at the memory. Then Mary realized thinking about her husband no longer brought an ache to her chest. She grabbed and squeezed Luke's hand. She'd taken Susan's advice and moved on.

Suddenly, she felt weak and beaten down by the recent events.

"Are you okay?" Luke's concerned voice came from a distance. "Mary." His strong arms picked her up and placed her in a kitchen chair. He brushed her hair out of her face.

A small glass of orange juice was placed in front of her by Special Agent Reese. "Here. Drink this. It should help."

"Thank you." She took a swallow and listened as Luke and the agent talked over her head.

She appreciated their concern but she really just needed a few minutes to recover before she answered any more questions. So she took her time sipping the juice. The poor teddy bear with its chest ripped by someone's attempt of intimidation brought more tears to her eyes. How silly, she was crying over a stuffed animal.

Holding the glass of juice in one hand, she dragged the teddy bear to her with the other. Without thought she tried to pinch together the cut material. Somehow, she would sew it back together.

She stuck her finger into the teddy bear to push the stuffing back in and her fingernail clicked on something. Unsure what it could be, she set her glass on the table and picked up the bear. With a little stuffing attached to it, she pulled out a flash drive.

"Whatcha' got there?" Special Agent Reese leaned over her shoulder to get a closer look.

She handed the flash drive over. "This must be the evidence Vincent hid."

The big man chuckled. "Just like in the movie when they hid the drugs in the doll." Reese held up the flash drive looking it over. "Instead your husband hid a hundred-twenty-eight gigabytes of evidence that will probably send our boy Lazaro away for a long time."

The FBI and their support people didn't leave until late afternoon. Thankfully, her laptop had not been damaged in any of the break-ins as by habit she'd hid it whenever she left the house. So they had used it to open up the flash drive. It hadn't been encrypted, and the special agent announced there appeared to be reams full of documents about money laundering, contracts on hits, and even several college football and basketball games where the *star players* were bribed to miss a few points. They were impressed by how Vincent had organized the information.

Mary happily watched their vans and SUVs disappear down the drive.

Before they left, Special Agent Reese had told them one of Chet's cousins worked for the same alarm company Mary had used for the house. Finally, that explained why their alarm was turned off every time they needed it. Another company located out of Birmingham was coming in next week to change it out. She wasn't taking any more chances.

Luke with the help of his dad re-hung the front door and nailed the frame back along with the backdoor, repairing the damage done by Chet and the armed agents bursting into the house. Jorge, his two bodyguards, along with Chet and his cousins were waiting in Sand City's jail for transport to Birmingham.

While Luke and his dad worked on patching the bullet holes in the walls, Mary answered the numerous voicemails from her mother. Once she explained what had happened and that everyone was okay, her mother declared she was finished with hospitals and ready to come home.

"Heaven knows, you need me there to watch out for you," her mom said.

Mary shook her head just thinking about it. Her mom was a force to be reckoned with and she could only hope to grow up to be just like her.

"We're picking up your mom tomorrow?"

Luke stood in the kitchen doorway, his hair mussed from working all afternoon. His dad and Sue Marie had worked alongside Luke and Mary to bleach blood stains out of the woodwork and then burn a couple of bloody area rugs. They'd wanted the house to be perfect before her mom came home.

She watched Luke, being sure to make mental pictures of him. More memories to revisit later. Men rarely stayed in her life long. Her dad had disappeared on a business trip when she was ten. Then, her mom's first boyfriend after her dad left. Mary had liked him a lot as he enjoyed playing board and card games with her. But after a couple of years he left and never returned, and then she decided to never let anyone else get close, out of fear of having her heart broken again. She had to admit Vincent leaving wasn't his fault, but she felt jinxed when it came to having a man in her life.

Dancing had been the center of her life. After Jorge hired her and she joined the dance line, men started sending her flowers and buying her expensive gifts. She had fun and even enjoyed an interesting sex life, but she never allowed a man to touch her heart. Until Vincent became part of her life.

Vincent had been her friend first and then later her

lover. When he decided he wanted her all to himself, he knew the only way he could do that was to place a ring on her finger. They had a huge fight about men flirting with her, but he kept telling her he loved her and wanted to marry her. It'd been hard to imagine anyone loving her, besides her mom. She'd finally agreed after six months. They had married in the local chapel with her mom and an Elvis impressionist as witnesses.

And now there was Luke. She was in love and it was totally unexpected. He acted like the bad boy on the outside but inside, and to all of those who loved him, he was a good man. That she knew for a fact.

With broad shoulders and chestnut hair brushing the nape of his neck, the man oozed sex appeal and danger. His five o'clock shadow gave him a scrumptious out-of-bed look. She liked it. No. She loved it. As she took in his dimpled grin and flashing blue eyes, she realized they needed to talk, to see if he had any deep feelings for her.

"Earth to Mary." Luke waved his hand in front of her face.

She slapped his hand away. "Stop that, silly."

Unable to resist, she let her fingers slide down his chest, feeling the firm muscles and warm flesh beneath his T-shirt. She'd never get tired of touching him.

"We need to talk." As soon as she said those words, Luke's face closed, stoic and ready to receive bad news. He tried to pull away and she cupped his beard-rough cheek. "Will you stay and protect me?"

"Have some of Jorge's cronies threatened you?" Concern wrinkled his forehead as he covered her hand with his.

"No. But you never can tell what I will get into next."

She stood on her tiptoes and kissed his lips. "I'm not very good at asking a man to come and live with me."

"So you want me to be your bodyguard?"

Was he being obtuse on purpose? Or did he plan to leave her? Frustrated, she decided a different tactic was called for. Subtlety wasn't working but she couldn't come out and say she loved him. Not counting the time between his changing her tire and becoming her handyman, they really had known each other for a short time. Rather ironic since they'd slept together within a few days he came to work for her.

"If you want to call yourself that you can. Or you could call yourself my live-in lover, my companion, my roommate—"

Chuckling, he placed his finger over her lips.

"I was teasing you," he said.

"Quit being a tease and answer me." She bit the tip of his finger before he moved it away.

"Ouch! You blood-thirsty woman."

He wrapped his arms around her body. She nestled in his arms, liking how right it felt.

When he still didn't say anything, she prodded. "Are you ever going to answer me?"

The smell of hard-working male brought the urge to rub her cheek against his chest. Oh, my goodness, she loved this man.

"No."

She froze. So. The sex had been great, but unless she was in a crisis or needy in some way, she was too boring to stick around. He would leave like all the men in her life had done. Taking a couple of deep breaths, she began filing away the memories. She'd gotten good at letting go. She would never want a man to stay because he felt sorry for her.

"All right then. I guess I'll go and pick up mom some her favorite snacks." She pulled away and started making busy work with her hands, folding a dish cloth, propping a glass inside the dishwasher. "Just lock up and turn on the alarm before you leave."

She was proud of how even her voice sounded. No tears spilling over, nothing on the outside for Luke to see how she was falling apart inside. She should've been an actress instead of a dancer.

"Wait." He caught her arm as she walked by.

Maintaining her indifferent attitude, with eyebrows raised, she looked into his eyes.

"Honey—"

"I know you don't remember me telling you this, but I prefer that you call me Mary." The hell with acting unconcerned. She was mad. She was tired of being dumped on by men.

"Why? Because your precious Vincent called you that?" An actual growl came out of Luke's mouth when he said it.

"No. Vincent called me Mary Katherine. He liked the sound. Occasionally, I'd dress up like a Catholic school girl for him. Some kinky hang-up about plaid skirts and white knee-high socks."

She wasn't sure why she told him that. She only knew she wanted him mad too. And from the look on his face, he was almost there.

Crossing her arms, she glared. "The person who started calling me Honey was Jorge. He picked me up off the streets at age sixteen when I ran away from home to Las Vegas. He was my lover and boss until he tired of me when I turned eighteen. Then he gave me to Vincent."

"I thought you and your mom moved to Las Vegas when you were a kid." He narrowed his eyes in disbelief.

"We actually moved to the suburbs, in Henderson, when we left Alabama. I ran away to the bright lights, to hide from my mom's last boyfriend. There's enough people and tourists on the crazy strip to get lost. I did what I thought necessary to survive and I don't have to explain anything to you."

With a shake of her head and a deep breath, she regained her composure.

"No, you don't. Though I believe I do. But first answer one more question. Did you love Vincent?"

She'd turned to leave the kitchen but that stopped her in mid-stride. One hand over her mouth, she turned to face Luke.

Her hand dropped to her side. "No. Not at first. But he loved me. I thought protection and someone taking care of me and my mom were enough. He worked hard to win my love and I did." She wanted to add, *but not like I love you.*

He nodded, staring at the floor as if he was looking for something to say.

All the built-up anger evaporated as she took a deep breath. "Listen, you don't need to explain anything to me. I understand circumstances brought us together and now it's over. We all need to get back to our own lives."

His head jerked up, eyes flashing.

"You think so, huh?" He crossed the space between them and picked her up by the upper arms and pushed her against the wall at eye level. At first, she struggled until he pressed his body to hers. As soon as his hips touched her stomach, he began to harden and she loved how his cock lengthened as he stared into her eyes. He grinned.

"You listen to me. I love you. I don't want to be just your

handyman, your protector, your lover, or your friend. I want to be all of those and your husband."

She wanted to shake her head to clear it, to make sure she'd heard right, but she was afraid he would misunderstand and think she was saying no.

She began to cry. Dear Lord, she cried too much around this man. Only this time it was from happiness.

"Aw, Mary, don't cry. Please tell me I didn't hurt you or scare you."

She shook her head. Thankfully, she had heard him correctly.

"I'm just so happy. I want those things too." She dug her fingers into his gorgeous chestnut hair and pulled his mouth to hers.

Oh my, Alabama boys know how to kiss.

Epilogue

O h no, not again.

"There goes that Luke Blackwood." The huff from the other side of the high-backed booth brought to mind the last time she found herself stuck in the same position with Betsy and Sue Marie at their gossiping best.

"Will he ever learn? Tsk-tsk." Sue Marie shook her head.

"He's going to hurt him if he doesn't watch it."

Luke was fighting again?

Mary looked out the diner's window and caught her husband juggling a diaper bag on one arm and nine-month-old Jacob on the other. She gasped, covering her mouth with both hands. Her graceful husband held tight to the squirming child and started toward the diner.

"You do have to say he's a fine daddy for Jacob. He goes nowhere without a new picture to show," Sue Marie said.

"So true. The reverend is so very proud of his son and positively dotes on his daughter-in-law and grandson. I even heard Mrs. Ford is helping out at the shelter. I know some of it is your sweet influence, Sue Marie."

Sue Marie giggled.

Betsy ignored her friend and continued. "They do make such a beautiful family. I just knew that one day Luke would grow out of his wild ways and make us all proud. You know the apple doesn't fall far from the tree and preachers' sons do make the best husbands."

The two older women sighed.

Though Mary agreed about preachers' sons, she was glad to disagree about Luke's growing out of his wild ways. She closed her eyes and remembered the night before after they had placed Jacob in bed, the wild things Luke had done to her brought a warmth to her cheeks.

"Now why is your mother's face so red? Has she been eavesdropping on Aunt Betsy and Aunt Sue Marie again?" Luke stood next to the booth, looking a little tired, but oh-so-handsome, holding a drooling child and a bright green bag. Nothing sexier than seeing the man she loved with what looked like mashed carrots on his chin. Well, except for last night; their new Jacuzzi tub was perfect for two. "Is Mommy embarrassed about being caught or is she thinking about bathtime already?"

"Luke," she whispered in admonishment. Then she cut her eyes over to the two ladies.

As she figured would happen, Betsy and Sue Marie now stood behind Luke, trying to tease a smile out of Jacob. Though not actually blood relatives, the two women had almost delivered Jacob when Mary's water broke in the middle of Lee's Dress and Store Barn and the situation progressed rather quickly by the time Luke pulled up to the hospital's ER.

Even Susan and Bubba had visited during her hospital

stay. Susan had opened a restaurant in Cullman, a city north of Birmingham, with the help of Bubba and his parents. Mary had been happy to hear her old friend was enjoying the same success she had in Sand City. Life had gotten better for her. In fact, a recent email had announced Susan was expecting Bubba Junior before Christmas.

Sue Marie held her hands out and Jacob fell into them.

"Just like his daddy. Never meets a woman he can't charm, especially the older ones," Mary said.

She grinned when she noticed Luke's face turning a little pink. The blushes started when he became a dad as he was near bursting with pride whenever someone bragged on his son.

As she stood next to Luke and talked about how many teeth Jacob had now, the new sheriff walked into the diner.

"Hey, J.T.," Luke said.

Mary smiled at the man once known as Evil.

He'd quit the FBI and decided to run for sheriff to replace Bubba. Though he'd cut his hair and hid his tattoos beneath a long-sleeve shirt, he still looked scary dangerous.

"I see you got squirt with ya." He ruffled Jacob's hair and nodded at the ladies. "How's your crop coming in this year?"

The two men stepped outside to talk about farming. J.T. owned a little land down the road from Mary's farm and often would come by to ask Luke questions. He never dated any of the single ladies that tried to draw his attention by speeding down Main Street. There was something sad about him and she felt like it wasn't only from his brother's death.

"Do you have any idea why J.T. is so sad?" she asked before thinking who she was asking.

Atlanta Edge Hockey Romance

Crossing The Line

Fake Play

Love In A Small Town Novels

Loving The Small-Town Preacher's Son

Loving The Small-Town Hero

Also by Carla Swafford

The Circle Organization

Circle of Desire

Circle of Danger

Circle of Deception

Circle of Dishonor (Novella)

Circle of Defiance (Novella

Kidnapped For A Day (Short Story)

A Southern Crime Family Novels

Jake

Sen (coming soon)

Ethan (coming soon)

Brothers of Mayhem Novels

Hidden Heat

Full Heat

Naked Heat

"Well, we better sit down. It'll take a while." Betsy scooted into the booth and waved Mary and Sue Marie in.

"Can we order more French fries?" Sue Marie asked. "These are cold now."

"Sounds like a good idea. How about you, Mary?" Ever since Betsy had become friends with her mother, she'd treated Mary with pleasant interest. She probably gossiped about her with Sue Marie, but as least she kept it in the family as Sue Marie had married the reverend last Christmas. And though she was now the step-grandmother to their son, out of respect to Luke and his mother, she asked them to call her aunt. What could a person say? Aunts in the South were as important as grandmothers. So Aunt Sue Marie she was.

"I'll have a Coke." She tugged out a bottle from the bag and handed it over for Sue Marie to feed her sweet boy.

"Let's see. Let's start with J.T.'s dad. He was the town drunk..."

Mary's eyes widened as Betsy told her all the gossip about the Rogan family and their run-in with the powerful Hicks family. Though the tale was interesting, her gaze kept drifting to the man she loved. He stood tall, talking with the sheriff. All his shadows were gone. He wasn't going anywhere without her. He loved her.

Sand City was as close to heaven as she'd ever get on earth.

About the Author

Carla Swafford loves romance novels, action/adventure movies, and men, and her books reflect that. And on top of it all, she's crazy about hockey, and thankfully, no one has made her turn in her Southern Belle card.

So, it's no surprise she writes spicy romantic suspense filled with mercenaries, motorcycle one-percenters, and southern criminals. And in the last few years, she's included sexy hockey players in books without suspense, except for the kind that asks, how will they ever find their happily ever after?